Goda Tales 5

Tales from a Desk at Home while Self-Isolating

Godalming Writers' Group

DEDICATION

For the residents, and our own hometown, of Godalming, nestled in the leafy suburbs of Surrey. And to all those writers, wherever they may be, trying to make a start. Keep trying. Your day will come.

And a big thank-you to the Godalming Museum Trust for details of events in Godalming's history from 820 AD onwards, to James Young for his work on the logo and not forgetting the Watts Gallery Trust for being such a creative inspiration to everyone that visits.

CONTENTS

INTRODUCTION

GODALMING: TOWN OF TALES AND LIGHT

by David Lowther

Godalming is about 4 miles south of Guildford with a population of twenty-one thousand. My wife and I came to live here three and a half years ago after moving from North East England. We arrived fairly familiar with the area since my late brother and his family have been resident here for donkey's years.

Those who have heard of Godalming (and there are plenty who haven't) but never visited probably think it to be a town of rich people driving expensive cars with the head of a typical family (2+2) commuting daily on crowded trains to London which is about 45 minutes away. That's not altogether true although the population growth of recent years is almost certainly due to more London-based workers moving in.

Godalming is part of the parliamentary constituency of Waverley and has, at the time of writing, a Tory MP, the famously mispronounced Jeremy Hunt of Radio 4 fame, whose recent failure to beat Boris Johnson to the keys to number 10 Downing Street has left him, for the time being, in political limbo. He has had time to open the newly constructed local flood defences and might, perhaps, squeeze in a meeting with the Godalming Writers' Group.

Godalming is undoubtedly a wealthy town and this can be confirmed by the number of large cars parked in the patrician supermarket compared with more modest vehicles in its proletarian equivalent not far away. But there are plenty of ordinary, easy-going, hard-working folk about. A strong sense of community is very evident and this is reflected in the large number of cultural and sporting activities (a vast majority of them are voluntary) which take place all year round. Chief among these (of course) is the Godalming Writers' Group (GWG), of which I'm proud to be a member.

Godalming Tales

Tales From a Couch in the Kings Arms

The Godalming Writers Group

The group dates back from 2015, before my arrival. Initially the enthusiastic members spent time chatting about their own writing experiences but soon they put together a series of short stories. Godalming Tales was published in 2017.

The GWG are a mixed bunch of men and women, schoolteachers, shopkeepers, bankers, IT specialists and retired people. What they share is the need to write so the publication of the first volume spurred them on to even greater efforts. Seeing the results of their labours in print resulted in a second volume which was published in late 2018. And this, the third set of stories is scheduled to hit the shelves in 2020.

Each tale shares certain characteristics; they are all about Godalming and the surrounding villages which the town serves and reflect the town's history, industry, education and diverse population. There's plenty of fun, a few gloomy moments, real people, fictional people, events that happened and some that didn't. Half-truths are everywhere; Godalming was the first place in the world to install electric street lighting (true) but that distinction was under threat from New York who sent a spy across the pond before the installation in the hope of stealing a march on the Surrey town (not true). The Russian Tsar Peter the Great stayed at the King's Arms in Godalming High Street in 1698 (true) but left without paying his bill (also true I'm told) but the King's Arms was not out of pocket (not true).

Jack Phillips, radio operator of the doomed Titanic, came from Godalming (true) and returned briefly as a ghost in the 21st century (er … not true). Then there's the legend of the Godalming teddy bears who live, love and flourish underground near the River Wey (true or false?)

Inevitably, nostalgia seeps out of some of the tales. 'Fings ain't what they used to be' Max Bygraves once sang and there are plenty of examples in the books, and in Godalming itself, as to how 'fings' have changed, and not always for the better. Once there were three cinemas and now there are none, although reasonably recent films are shown at the Borough Hall at weekends. And there is a brilliant film society which screens films in the

Borough Hall throughout the autumn, winter and spring.

Godalming Tales Vol. 2

Tales from a table in the Jack Phillips

The Godalming Writers Group

Where once there were two railway stations there is now but one, although a further three serve the outlying villages. A fair number of celebrities were born in and around the town. Amongst them were Julius Caesar (the Surrey cricketer not the Roman dictator), Mick Mills (Ipswich and England footballer), Aldous Huxley and Ben Elton. Godalming was the most frequently mentioned settlement in the Reginald Perrin novels and Charterhouse School is the Alma Mater of Jeremy Hunt, Peter May (great cricketer) and Simon Raven (very funny writer). Many of the stories in Godalming Tales are themselves amusing, others laced with irony, some sad and one or two even macabre.

The town is a place of huge contrasts and has wide differences in the cross-section of its population. There are the incomers, folk who work in London but can't buy a house near to the capital due to the crazy property prices there, farmers, office workers, plenty of small shopkeepers, teachers and other public servants.

Reading Godalming Tales is far more interesting than ploughing through some dusty history book. The town is surrounded by reminders of the Second World War, especially Wanborough Manor near Puttenham where SOE agents were trained before being parachuted into occupied Europe. It's a fascinating place, well worth a visit and the three volumes of Godalming Tales serve as an absorbing introduction to the town.

REVISITING THE WATTS

by Ian Honeysett

It had been many years since my last visit to the Watts Gallery in Compton. But my wife was away on a Croquet tournament and I was feeling at something of a loose end. I had recently injured my ankle when trying to exit the rowing machine at Broadwater Leisure Centre; my 'go-to' place for keeping fit. So, my ankle was now encased in a rather impressive support. I decided to make a return visit to a place we had often visited when our children were growing up. As I sat on the no 46 bus to Compton, pleasant images filled my mind. I recalled the very first time we went there, back in 1983 I think it was. Before we had children in fact. The Gallery had opened in 1904, just before the celebrated Victorian artist, George Frederick Watts, had died leaving his artist wife, Mary, to look after it all. A task she did very well as the Gallery survived as one of the few galleries in the UK dedicated to the work of a single artist.

But by 1983, I recalled, it certainly looked its age. Crumbling masonry, dark and damp was my abiding memory. On the other hand, it was also free to enter which meant it became a popular place for us to take visiting friends to if it was raining.

I remembered the way in to the Gallery took you past a shop that sold paintings and, my favourite, a shop that stocked a huge variety of teas. I love tea.

The room resonated with the glorious aroma of tea. It was there that I discovered Russian Gunpowder tea (at least I think that's what it was called). So, having stocked up with a range of loose teas, we would make our way to the Gallery itself. We had never seen a building quite like it. We'd done our research and knew it had been designed by one Christopher Hatton Turnor who was an admirer of Edwin Lutyens (whom we *had* heard of). It was inspired by the Arts and Crafts movement; simple, traditional craftsmanship. Lots of medieval and folk styles. Flowers. Leaves. Plenty of leaves. We'd read that one key feature was that there were top-lit galleries which meant that the paintings could be viewed under natural light. And it was on our doorstep too.

One vivid memory was of when we took the children there and they quickly made friends with the then-Curator, Richard Jeffries', children. It was always entertaining when he was there as he often demonstrated his large collection of old gramophones and phonographs. On one occasion he played us a wax cylinder of Sir Arthur Sullivan conducting one of his overtures as the children happily raced around the gallery and disappeared behind one particularly big painting which stood out from the wall. Our hearts missed a beat as we had visions of them all bursting out through the canvas. However, I don't think they ever did. Clearly, they all appreciated great art.

I pictured us on our very first visit, pushing open the front door of the Gallery and finding ourselves in what looked like a sitting room. A very large sitting room admittedly. There was an old sofa to our left, covered in newspapers. A half-drunk cup of tea on a small coffee table. (Why is a coffee table generally small and a tea-table large? Just asking). We were beginning to wonder if this was, indeed, the Gallery or was it, perhaps, the Curator's house? Had we gone a building too far? But then a voice soon put us straight.

'Welcome to the Watts Gallery,' it announced. 'Is this your first visit?' We looked up at a very tall, gangling figure draped in an old cardigan. And wearing carpet slippers. He had one of those faces that looked permanently etched with a smile. 'My name is Wilfred Blunt,' he added. 'I am the Curator.' He grinned and immediately we felt welcome. It was all very informal. He might even have asked if we'd like a cup of tea? In fact, he probably didn't as I would almost certainly have said 'yes' but I don't recall sitting on that sofa and supping.

'Would you like me to show you around the Gallery?' he enquired.

'Why that would be very kind of you,' we both replied. 'But we don't want to put you to any trouble.'

'No trouble at all,' he replied jovially. 'I've finished the paper so I'm quite free.' He then proceeded to show us the paintings. Such a variety: portraits, landscapes and what might be called symbolic. Lots of figures from Greek and Roman mythology. Most of them we'd never heard of. They were quite big. Some were very big. A few were enormous. To be honest, they were not necessarily pictures we would have hung on our walls – had the walls been big enough of course. One that particularly struck us was of a drowned woman under an arch by the River Thames. Quite an unusual subject we thought.

'It's called 'Found Drowned', observed Mr Blunt. 'Watts famously said that he painted ideas, not things.'

'An apt title,' agreed my wife. 'It makes you think.'

'George Frederick would have been delighted to hear you say so,' replied Mr Blunt.

We smiled at each other, happy at the thought that we would have pleased the artist who has been called 'England's Michelangelo', so varied was his output of both paintings and sculptures.

*****

'Watts Gallery!' declared the bus driver. I awoke from my reverie and cautiously shuffled off the bus. I had my walking stick for support as I crossed the road and made my way to the Visitor Centre. Oh, this was all so new! A Visitor Centre indeed. I looked around the bustling shop full of books and postcards and Watts' memorabilia. And, not surprisingly, I saw I now had to buy a ticket! No more free art. I noticed, though, that there was a free exhibition upstairs. But was it wise for me to attempt the stairs given my ankle? I looked around in case

4

there was a lift or escalator but neither presented itself. So, clutching my ticket, I headed for the Gallery. Was that old tea shop still there? My pulse quickened but it was not. There was a Tea Room so I made a mental note to look in later. As I turned the corner past some pleasant flower beds and Arts and Crafts signs recalling Patrons of the Gallery, I noticed a door proclaiming an 'Artist in Residence'. Interesting. But then I saw a sign revealing that, today, they were residing elsewhere. Disappointing. I'd never met an Artist in Residence.

I passed through the gate and turned to face the Gallery full on. If only I had brought my sketchbook with me, I could have sat and drawn the scene. Triangular shapes predominated. Each housed a window with brilliant green tiles. And there were now beautifully tended flowers and bushes everywhere. I was fairly sure it didn't look like this in the 'old' days.

I pushed open the new front door of the Gallery and was met with a cheery 'Welcome to the Watts!' But this wasn't Wilfred Blunt (who died in 1987, so just as well) but a charming lady with a name badge and broad smile. I showed her my ticket. I noticed she had a walkie-talkie. Very professional.

'Have you been here before?' she asked.

'Oh yes, but many years ago. I see you've removed the sofa.'

She looked nonplussed.

'It's just that, when I first came here, Wilfred Blunt was the Curator and his sofa was just there.'

She smiled again and explained the new layout of the Gallery. It all looked so smart and bright. And air-conditioned. Only the paintings appeared to be the same. Except now there was a Special Exhibition too of an artist I hadn't quite heard of. And there were cards in each part of the Gallery with details of the paintings. Not the same as Mr Blunt's personal explanations but possibly more reliable.

As I surveyed the paintings, I was delighted to see that the 'Drowned Woman' was still there. And the famous painting of 'Hope' – the blind female sitting on the globe with a one-stringed lyre. Apparently, President Obama's favourite. And, yes, there was my personal choice, the portrait of Rachel Gurney which King Edward VII had wanted to buy but Mary Watts had refused him. Which was a fairly unusual experience for Teddy. I'd always enjoyed Watts' portraits, for which he was famous of course. Especially Rachel.

But my ankle was starting to hurt now and I wasn't too sure about descending the stairs to see the Special Exhibition and Watts' sculptures. And I really wanted to see what had happened to the old Sculpture Gallery. In those days, it was like going down into a mine. Ill-lit and wet. We used to joke with the children that, at least, it had running water. You had to tread carefully as the floor was littered with stones and bits of sculpture. I needed to see whether they had tidied everything up. And were those massive figures still there? The man on a horse. Physical Energy. I'd seen a bronze of it in Kensington Gardens a year or two back and it was very impressive. As was the statue of Lord Tennyson. Someone had told me that it was popularly known as 'the Cabbie's Lament' as he is looking at something in his hand. A desultory tip no doubt. Then I noticed there was a lift. I stepped inside. Just one floor so it wouldn't take long. There was a button on the wall which I pressed and I started to descend. And then suddenly stopped. Odd. Was I there already? Surely not. Had they installed a high-speed lift? I tried the door but it held fast. I was stuck! Trapped! 'Hello?' I said. 'Hello, anyone there?' I repeated rather more loudly.

'You need to keep your finger on the button!' came the reply.

'Oh, sorry,' I answered. I duly pressed the button until there was a click. And, this time, the door did open. But what confronted me was not what I expected at all! It was sombre and gloomy and smelt strongly of damp. Surely, they hadn't left this part of the Gallery untouched? The part that most needed changing?

I looked around and could just make out a tall, gangling figure.

'Are you all right? You just need to remember to keep pressing the button!'

'I say,' I said, 'you look just like Wilfred Blunt!'

'Of course I do. I am Wilfred Blunt. Have we met?'

This was extraordinary. The volunteer was not only called Wilfred Blunt but looked just like him!

'You look a trifle confused, old chap. Now I come to think about it, I believe we have met. You came here with your charming wife just a few weeks ago. Is that right?'

'Well, not just a few week… we met you back in… it must be 1983 I think.'

'That's right – a few weeks ago as I said. And, by the way, it still is 1983 as far as I am aware!' he laughed. 'When did you think it was?'

'Oh, this is very odd,' I replied, somewhat confused. 'Have I hit my head or something? Is this a joke? Is this a new Gallery attraction: revisit the Gallery as it was before the renovations?'

'I must confess, I have no idea what you're on about, old chap,' replied Wilfred. 'There's been no renovation here, I'm afraid, though it is sorely needed. The damp is certainly doing my health no good at all.'

'Do you mind if I take a look in the Sculpture Gallery?' I asked hesitantly.

'Gallery might be a rather grand term for it,' he laughed again. 'But come with me and tread carefully. I keep meaning to tidy up but just never have the time. It's rather appealing, don't you think?'

There was no mistaking the two huge figures of Tennyson and Physical Energy.

'Yes, there are three castings of Energy you know: in Cape Town, Harare and Kensington Gardens.'

'And a fourth to be erected around Compton,' I blurted out, having read about it quite recently.

'Oh, I don't think so, old chap. There's no money for that I'm afraid. An excellent idea though. But, look, would you care for a cup of tea? You don't look quite right if I might say so.'

'Well, I never refuse a cup of tea, Mr Blunt. That's very kind of you.'

He got into the lift with me and pressed the button.

'So, when was the lift installed?' I enquired. 'I don't recall it being here when I last visited.'

'Oh, it wasn't,' he replied somewhat ambiguously.

How, I asked myself, would he explain all the renovations upstairs? But, when the lift door opened, it was apparent that there had been no work done here at all. All was rather faded and had clearly seen better days. Quite dark despite those top-lit windows.

'Do sit down, old chap, and I'll make you some tea. Do you take milk and sugar?'

'Just milk, please.'

I sat down on the sofa. As before, it was covered with newspapers. I picked one up. It was The Times dated 22 July 1983 and announced 6p off income tax. John Le Carre's 'The Little Drummer Girl' was the latest best-seller. My brain started to hurt. I had surely gone back in time! Either that or this was an exact recreation of the old Watts Gallery. And why would they do that?

Wilfred Blunt ambled back with my tea.

'Sorry I spilt some in the saucer but I'm not as steady as I once was. I am in my 80s after all.'

I drank the remains of the tea. If this person was an actor then here was my opportunity to test him.

'It must have been quite a shock when your brother, Anthony, the Royal Art Adviser no less, admitted to being a Russian spy?' I said.

'Not really,' he replied. 'I always suspected something was not quite right about him. He finally admitted it in 1964 but I had my suspicions well before then. Went to Cambridge you know. Say no more, I'm an Oxford man.'

I really didn't know what to do next. If I left the Watts now, would I be returning to Godalming in 1983? Would I relive my life since then? Could I change things? What would I change? My mind was in complete turmoil. My brain began to hurt even more.

'You really don't look well,' said Mr Blunt – or Wilfred as I thought of him now, we had drunk tea

10

together. But how to reply? If this was all real then should I tell him I was from the future? Surely not wise as he looked so ancient, he might well have a coronary.

'It's been really enjoyable seeing you again after all… these couple of weeks,' I replied at length. 'But I had better be getting back home. Don't want to miss my bus.'

'You're always welcome,' he smiled. 'It would be good to have more visitors. Perhaps one day we will be able to restore the place to its former glory. But probably not in my day.'

I got up with some difficulty from the settee which was quite low down. And then my stick somehow got caught between my feet and I felt myself falling. Then everything went black.

'I say, are you OK? You've had a bit of a fall.'

I looked up. It was the very pleasant lady on the door. She looked most concerned.

I smiled back.

'No, I'm fine,' I replied. 'Not quite used to this stick.'

'I can't see a cut but I suspect you may have a bit of a bruise tomorrow. Are you sure you're all right?'

'Don't worry,' I said. 'It's been quite an afternoon. I think, maybe, I just need a nice cup of tea.'

NOSTALGIA GAMES
by Pauline North

'Sorry was that your foot?'

'That's alright – Fi? Fiona Baker? It is isn't it?'

'Well I'm blowed, Maggie Abbott, fancy meeting you here, are you running in this too? I seem to remember you hated sports at school.'

'After all those years who would believe we would meet again here, at the inaugural Godalming half marathon of all places, how did we manage it in a crowd like this? Have you moved back here? I never knew where you had moved to.'

'No, I don't live here; I have been working here, I'm only here for a couple of weeks though, helping out in the local office.'

'How much longer can they keep us waiting, I'm getting tired just standing here.'

'I know what you mean this is a bit of a crush. Oh, here we go. Let's take it easy, pace ourselves. Do you still see anyone from those days, Peter Denton perhaps?'

'Look over there, all those people waving, just like the London marathon.'

'You really liked him, do you remember that end of term dance, you hung around him all evening, he was so embarrassed he had to leave in the end.'

'That wasn't because of me; he left with you because you made him an offer he couldn't refuse.'

'Really?'

'So everyone said.'

'Only after you spread that story about.'

'It was a long time ago Fiona, we were very young, let it go.'

'What do you do with yourself these days Maggie, are you married, where do you work?'

'I work for the council, in the housing department. What do you do?'

'I'm an accountant. I was married, ten years we were together, I was pregnant but I lost her when I found out he was having an affair. Three months later he died.'

'I'm sorry.'

*****

'If we jog any slower, we'll be walking.'

'It doesn't matter as long as we finish. Almost everyone has moved away, the town has changed a lot in the last few years, even our old school. A few of us still get together sometimes, have a few drinks in The Star, talk over the past.'

'He came back.'

'Who did?'

'Peter Denton.'

'Back to Godalming?'

'Back for me. We have been together for months now; I didn't think I would ever feel this happy. He travels all over for his company and is away a lot. He's so sweet, he says he misses me so much it is easier if he doesn't contact me while he's away. Before he went this time, he promised to make it the last time, he's going to hand in his notice when he comes back and find a job locally, then we can get married.'

'When do you expect him to return?'

'I haven't heard from him for a while, I expect he's very busy but he promised to be home in time for us to marry before Christmas.'

'And you are planning ahead for that, to be ready when he comes back?'

'Yes, I waited so long for him I don't mind holding on a little longer.'

*****

'How much further is it do you think?'

'I think we are about halfway, we're almost back to the Borough hall, then one more circuit. Are you feeling alright Maggie, you look pale as a ghost?'

'Do I? I'm only puffed, I think I'll walk for a while.'

'Good idea, I'll walk with you, is this your first time, doing a run like this?'

'Yes.'

'Did you have a check-up at your doctor's, to make sure your heart and everything are up to this? You look awful.'

'Do I? No, I didn't think I would need to. Do I really look bad?'

'Honest, I'm not sure you should carry on.'

'Now you mention it should my heart be beating like this when we're moving so slow? I don't feel very well at all.'

'Stop a minute, let me feel your pulse. Now that is seriously fast. Look my car is parked just down that road over there. Why don't you let me take you home? There will be other chances to run, after you have seen a doctor.'

'Would you? I would be very grateful; we could have a cup of tea and continue catching up.'

'Come on it's this one over here. That door needs a good slam I'm afraid, that's right, now if you can direct me to your place.'

'Of course, it is quite simple from here actually, take the first left, next right, right again. Now left and my place is the one by the bus stop.

'Come in, it isn't very tidy I'm afraid. Do you want to come in the kitchen while I make the tea?'

'You have a very cosy home, Peter must find it very welcoming when he comes back, a real sanctuary.'

'Oh yes, he says all he wants is to come back to me so we can spend the rest of our lives together. Did you ever think when we were at school, and you were the one he wanted because you were blonde and pretty and I was the dull plain girl in the corner that everyone ignored, that I would be the one to win his love?'

'I don't suppose I gave it a thought; life has a way of turning things upside down doesn't it.'

'Yes, I'm sorry I didn't think, you have had a rough time of it. Would you like to see some photos of me and Peter, see how he's changed over the years? I have them in this album, let's sit on the sofa and I can talk you through them.'

'Lovely shall I put my tea down here?'

'Here we are, I'm pretty O.C.D I'm afraid I have organised them all in sequence, first to last. This is the first one; I used a selfie stick so we could both be in it. I could hardly hold it still; I can't tell you what he was doing with his hands.'

'You're both wearing winter coats in this one, when was this taken?'

'Boxing day, he had to spend Christmas day with his mum, she's on her own, so he made it up to me the next day, made it really special. This next photo is just Peter and I think it shows him well, what do you think? I think he looks even better now, with a bit of maturity.'

'Where was this one taken? It's later in the year isn't it?'

'It was that warm spell we had in April, in Bognor; we had two whole days there. And as for this one, I don't know if I should show you this one, Peter wanted a special photo of me, it is a little bit naughty but he loves it.'

'Do you know what? I think I forgot to lock my car; I was so concerned that you were all right when we got here. I won't be a minute and then we can look through the rest.

*****

'That was quick, look at this one Fi… what? Why have you got that rope? Don't! Leave me alone! Is this some sort of game? Owww. That hurts, you cow! HELP!!'

'Just shut up! Ok, I'm going to have to stuff something in that stupid mouth. There! Now I'm just going to make sure my knots are secure and you can't move, then you can listen to me, right!

'You were so busy boasting about your perfect little life, how you nailed the school stud, eventually, when he was losing his hair and his looks and his marriage had become a little dull and likely to get worse because his stupid wife had gone and got pregnant. The way married life can go, for a while, after ten years.

17

'Do I see a little tiny glimmer of realisation? You didn't ask my name. Do you want to know my married name? Well, you dull, boring little frump, my name for the last ten years and three months has been Denton, Fiona Denton.

'It was a wonderful marriage, ups and downs of course that happens in every relationship. When I got pregnant, he panicked. He had never imagined himself as a father, like a lot of men. He would have got past that if you hadn't tracked him down, oh I know you did. You latched on to him at the perfect time; you were a little light relief.

'Christmas day he was with me, every time he told you he was away working he was with me. And then one day I found out about you, I found an email on his laptop, you had even attached a disgusting photo. I walked out of our bedroom to go downstairs, I was crying, my eyes full of tears. I tripped and fell all the way down the stairs, I was on my own. I lost my baby.

'Now, I am going to put these gloves on and wipe clean every surface I have touched in here and put my cup away. By the way the car is Peter's, did you notice I put gloves on to drive? No? I don't think anyone saw us come in but to be on the safe side I will wait until after dark, then if I'm careful no-one will see us leave.

'If I was you, I would stop snivelling you'll only block up your nose and then how will you breathe?

'I am going upstairs now to arrange your bedroom, find your passport, remove some of your stuff, things a woman would take if she was running away with a married man. Leave doors and drawers open as if you were in a rush, drop some pretty pants on the floor. You see I am going to be kind; the two of you can be together, for eternity. They are building a new flyover, quite near to home and there's a great big pit just waiting for the concrete that will be poured in tomorrow. They will find Peter's car, abandoned – well you don't need to know where, do you? Nothing can save you now.'

Godalming Events

Victorian 1870 – 1901
1885 – Grammar School set up in hall beside the Red Lion.
1872 – Charterhouse School moved from London to Godalming.
1870 – Godalming Voluntary Fire Brigade established.

HUMPHREY, JEFFREY AND GODFREY: THE HAIRCUT

by Martyn MacDonald-Adams

'So, how would you like me to trim it?'

Humphrey felt a little uneasy sitting under a thick blanket on a high chair in Woof's tree house. He stared into the mirror at, what seemed to him, a maniacal dog-barber about to decapitate an innocent teddy bear with a pair of scissors. He started to regret accepting his friend's offer to make him look sexier.

Woof snipped eagerly at the air.

'Err, a little off the top, a little off the sides and off the collar. Just tidy it up.'

Woof nodded. 'And the other ear?'

(Snip, snip)

'Ear? Are you hinting I've got hairy ears?'

'Nooooo. No, no, no. Not hinting at all. I'm telling you; your ears *are* hairy.'

(Snip, snip, snip).

Humphrey sighed. Woof was, in fact, correct. Then again, all teddy bears have hairy ears. His had been just a little more 'enthusiastic' in that department recently.

'Yours are worse!' Humphrey grumbled back and wincing as Woof continued to snip-away at nothing in particular.

(Snip, snip, snip).

'Ah, but woofs like me are considered handsome if we have thick hairy ears.' And so, he started trimming the bear's flappy bits. A split second after each snip Humphrey's ear would twitch involuntarily but Woof soon got into the rhythm of things and slowly but surely, they were neatly trimmed.

The would-be barber then moved on to tidy up the rest of the teddy bear's head and then gently trim his eye brows. It didn't take long for, although Humphrey was hairy, it was teddy-bear hair and it never grew too long or too wild. Not for Humphrey anyway, but he knew that female teddy bears could be much more critical.

Earlier in the week, Woof had been trotting down Godalming's High Street when he'd seen the local barbers at work in their shop. He'd sat outside and watched, fascinated by the skill of the hair dressers. Now he wanted to try out this new knowledge on someone and a teddy bear in need of a tidy up was a perfect candidate.

'I think I need to tackle those small, difficult to cut, fuzzy hairs,' said Woof, peering inside Humphrey's left ear. He put down his scissors, reached to one side and produced a short metal rod with a cotton tip. Then, he opened a small metal bottle of something and dipped the tip of the rod inside before deftly striking a match and lighting the end. Humphrey's eyebrows rose a little in surprise. Woof then gently 'whapped' the side of Humphrey's ear with the fiery tip and a small crinkly flame shot up and instantly vanished.

In one instant he'd eradicated all those little hairs that are too bothersome to trim.

It happened so fast that Humphrey didn't have time to scream. But now his left ear was warm. Very warm, but also quite comfy-warm. Outwardly he was still half-way toward full-blown panic with eyes and mouth making large O shapes. As he paused to ponder this event Woof 'whapped' the other ear and another crinkly flame shot up and vanished. Humphrey now had two very, very warm ears and two very, very close brushes with a fiery demise.

On the plus side, not one of those all-but-invisible hairs remained.

'Are you trying to set me on fire?'

'Don't be silly. I saw the barbers in the High Street do it – although, come to think of it, when *they* do it there's no sheet of flame.'

'You don't say!'

'If you let those little hairs grow again, I reckon that would be a neat trick for fireworks night. Don't you think?'

'No, it wouldn't! Stop it!'

Woof examined Humphrey's nose.

'Do you have hairy nostrils?'

'No! Look, I came here for a trimming not a toasting. What would you have done if I had caught fire?'

'Oh, don't worry. My little tree house would be just fine. That's a fire blanket you're wearing. You see? I thought of everything. I even have a bucket of water beside us, just in case.'

'Oh,' said Humphrey.

'So, tell me, what's all this trimming for? You have a date with a lady bear perhaps?'

'Family visit.'

'Product?'

'Prod who?'

'Would sir like some product? I don't have much to offer but I have a fresh air spray, a jelly in the fridge and maybe a jar of Vaseline somewhere.'

'Fresh hair sounds good. Thanks.'

Woof went to the lavatory and returned with a spray can.

'When you said fresh...'

Woof sprayed at Humphrey's head.

'Ah... ah... ahtchoo!'

'There you are, smelling like a pile of clean linen. Just like my nice clean lavatory. Hot towel?'

'I'be dod wed.'

'Pardon?'

'I'be dot wet!'

'You're not wet. No, but my mirror is,' said Woof peering at the spatter on his mirror. 'I'll have to clean it now. The next time I trim you, remind me to fit a windscreen wiper on my mirror first. By the way, the kettle is boiled and the hot towel is steamed. It feels wonderful; opens your pores. Would you like to try it...?'

'My paws are fine, thanks.'

In fact, Humphrey's paws were still clenching the arms of the chair from fear.

Woof held up a hand mirror so that the bear could see the back of his head. Thankfully it looked pretty much as it did before. No sign of singed hair.

'How much do I owe you?' asked Humphrey as he clambered down to the floor making a silent resolution never to do this again.

'Three will do.'

Humphrey handed over three chocolate biscuits then broke a chocolate bourbon in half and gave it to Woof as a tip. He ate the other half, mainly to calm his nerves.

'Thank you,' smiled Woof and put them into his new biscuit tin making a quiet 'Kerching!' sound to himself.

It was raining outside so Humphrey put his child-face mask on, the one that, from a distance, and to a very short-sighted person, made him *almost* look like a very young human, albeit one with a big nose. He then grabbed his child's plastic rain coat, put the hood up and pulled on his miniature bright red wellingtons. Basically, he'd copied the idea from an illegal immigrant from Peru, but the face mask was all his. The number of opticians in Godalming's High Street is testimony as to how short sighted the locals are.

He bid Woof a hearty farewell and set off along the river path toward his secret home under the Godalming Bowling Club.

Humphrey would never admit it but he loved the rain, and being dressed as a child was a really good excuse to stamp in all the puddles along the way. Not everything humans did was silly. In his view, the older humans got, the sillier they became. It was the older ones that had invented things like mortgage repayments, wars and parking tickets. He wondered why they thought they were so intelligent.

But, to his surprise, he found himself already missing that cosy warm-ear feeling. It had been a really, really nice feeling. So much so, he wondered when he'd have the courage to live dangerously and have another one of Woof's haircuts. Fireworks night maybe?

Provided Woof had a bucket of water nearby.

THE EMERGENCY PANTS
by Paul Rennie

One minute he was walking past the Sun pub, where Wharf Street meets Godalming High Street, the next he was lying on his back on the cobblestones in the middle of the road. His head felt fuzzy and he couldn't remember how he got there. All he knew was that the cobblestones didn't make a very comfortable mattress, but this was as nothing compared to the pain in his leg. It seemed to be at a funny angle and he couldn't move it. The back of his head also throbbed and he couldn't think straight. As his vision cleared a little, he could see quite a crowd of people peering down at him. Some were looking sympathetic and reaching down to help him, some were merely ogling a fellow human being in distress as a way to brighten up their day and give them something to talk about in the pub, but his eyes were drawn to a girl with a pony tail, in a blue top and black leggings who had her mobile phone out. At first, he thought she was calling for an ambulance, but then he realized she was holding it out towards him and was filming him lying there. He had heard about people who did this, and that the video was likely to end up on YouTube to be viewed by millions for entertainment.

He tried to put it out of his head, as he had more important things on his mind, and needed to concentrate on how he had got into this situation. His thoughts were flashing around like stroboscopic lights, and they wouldn't organize themselves into something coherent, only unconnected fragments. He remembered stepping off the pavement and thinking that he only needed to look left because of the one-way system. Then something had hit his leg and hip very hard, knocking him over. Something red – a car. He now had a recollection of a man in a hat behind the windscreen, his face aghast and frozen in horror as he gripped the wheel, but unable to turn it, nor brake. So he had been run over, and that would explain why his leg hurt terribly, and why he couldn't move. A kindly middle-aged woman with a concerned expression touched him on the shoulder and asked if he was all right, but he couldn't clear his head to speak. He knew that there was something important he needed to remember and, in particular, to work out why he was in town and where he had been heading.

A few more recollections came into his head. He had been on his way to the bus stop in Bridge Street, but where was he going and why? That was it, he was trying to catch the 10.57 Number 70 bus to Guildford, which meant it was for something that he couldn't get in Godalming, something special. But what was it? His mind's eye scanned the shops in Guildford. Not the Friary, even though it was closest to the bus station, nor was it Tunsgate, far too expensive for his tastes. He traced the route up the High Street, and, about a third of the way up, on the left, there it was. For some reason he had been on his way to Marks & Spencer. It had been many years since he had visited that emporium, but, as more memories came back, he recalled that he had gone there in the past to buy underpants, and that today he had been on his way to buy some new ones. But why was that important and nagging at him when he had his leg to worry about?

*****

Another memory came flooding back from that shopping trip all those years ago. This time he was in the men's' underwear section at M&S, and he recalled being overwhelmed by the different shapes, styles, sizes and colours. In the end he'd chosen a pack of three of what were called slips, which were one of the smaller styles and a little more racy than briefs, mainly because they looked quite good on the mannequin. When he tried them on at home, they didn't look quite as flattering as they had in the store display, and were a bit snugger and a tad more revealing than he had expected, but he was too embarrassed to take them back, mainly because it might mean convincing the shop assistant that he hadn't worn them. His mother was even less enthusiastic. 'Why did you buy white ones? You should have bought coloured patterned ones; white pants are an accident waiting to happen.' But he had laughed, telling her that all the male film stars seemed to wear white pants. 'Well they can afford new ones every day,' she had retorted.

Over the years the pants gave good service, although had obviously deteriorated and, unlike a fine wine, hadn't improved with age. One of the pairs of the original threesome had parted company with its elastic waist and had been regenerated as a duster. Another pair had mysteriously vanished, possibly down the back of the immersion heater, along with a few odd socks and flannels. The final pair remained resolutely in circulation, long past their design life. Over the years fashions and materials had changed, but these antique pants remained in service, a credit to past quality standards. They had become a grey/yellow colour, mainly from mishaps in the washing machine, sharing dyes with more colourful clothing. The elastic on the legs and waist had become loose and baggy, stretched as his waist expanded over the years, so that they could no longer take up the slack and, like its sibling, the waistband had started to separate. Worse still, they had developed a hole, which on occasions exposed parts they were supposed to cover.

His mother had threatened to throw them out on many occasions, but he insisted on keeping them as his emergency pair, for use only when there were no more clean ones in the drawer. She warned him many times, 'Don't go out in those pants, you might get run over, and then the doctors and nurses would see them.' But he had laughed at her, telling her that it was an old wives' tale, and that it would never happen.

His mind drifted back to his current situation. So, he had been on his way to Guildford M&S to buy some new underpants. That was ok then, nothing important. In the background he could hear the sound of an ambulance arriving. 'At last,' he thought, 'I'm being taken care of, and I'll soon be off these uncomfortable cobbles.' The two paramedics in their green overalls knelt down and checked him carefully, reassuring him that everything would be all right. He started to relax, and then the final piece of the jigsaw of his returning memory shot into his brain like a bolt of lightning. *He was wearing his emergency underpants*, not only that, the reason he was wearing them was that he hadn't got round to washing his other pairs, and that had been five days ago.

The reassuring voice of the young lady paramedic spoke into his ear, 'You've been in an accident and you've hurt your leg. We are going to have to cut your trousers off to get a better look at the damage.'

Behind her, the girl with the ponytail and mobile phone camera leaned forward.

Godalming Events

Post-War 1948 – 1964

1964 – Godalming High Street renumbered.

1954 – The Round Table founded.

1953 – Godalming and Districts Scouts formed.

1952 – Winkworth Arboretum passed to National Trust by Wilfred Fox.

1950 – Godalming United Football Club formed by former pupils of Godalming Grammar School.

1948 – Austin Playfoot of Eashing ran with the Olympic torch from Merrow to Guildford.

SKULDUGGERY ON THE 9:09 TO PORTSMOUTH

by Alan Barker

June 1905

He watched the train approach, steam billowing from its chimney and around its wheels. Gradually it slowed and ground to a halt.

A door was opened and a petite lady wearing a frilly white blouse and bell-shaped skirt stepped gingerly on to the platform. Lewis Pomfret - Louis, to his friends and foes alike - grabbed her cases from the train and passed them to her, tipping his cap and grinning like a mischievous monkey. She gave him a quizzical look and hurried off.

Lewis had spent the previous evening at Archie Wright's house, playing poker until after midnight - quite profitably as it happened - before snatching a few hours' sleep on his friend's sofa followed by a bath and a hearty breakfast.

Feeling flush in more ways than one, he'd been able to afford a second-class ticket, Lewis hopped on the train and stood gazing out at the Surrey town of Woking before it gradually disappeared from view. He'd enjoyed his evening with Archie and friends but was now looking forward to getting back home to Portsmouth.

He wandered along the corridor peering into the compartments before entering one which held two occupants: a man sitting by the door and another near the window.

Lewis took a seat and settled down for the journey. Despite his lean frame he had a voracious appetite and was soon digging into his jacket pocket for his liquorice allsorts.

His gaze flitted over the scenic pictures below the luggage-racks but after a while he surreptitiously surveyed his fellow passengers. Observing strangers was one of his favourite ways of passing time; it often paid dividends during poker, he'd found.

The gentleman sitting opposite was immersed in the Daily Chronicle, peering at it through the pince-nez perched on his nose. Occasionally he rummaged in his pocket and helped himself to a pinch of snuff. A rum cove, Lewis decided.

The man seated by the window seemed to be asleep. His hands were neatly folded in his lap and his knees rested together. His jacket and trousers were somewhat dishevelled as if he had spent the night in them. A top hat rested lightly on his head.

Shortly the train slowed as they approached Guildford. The snuff-taking gentleman folded his newspaper crisply and reached up for his briefcase and bowler before disembarking, and was soon lost in the crowd on the platform.

Lewis gazed at the door expecting other passengers to enter the compartment but nobody did so. The train lurched forward and headed into the Surrey countryside once more. Minutes later they arrived at Farncombe station which was considerably quieter than Guildford. Still no one came into the compartment.

As the train moved off again Lewis got to his feet, stretched his arms as if exercising, and stepped softly towards the gentleman by the window. Leaning down, he placed his hand in front of the man's face and made a quick movement. Nothing. Sleeping like a log, he thought.

Rolling up his sleeve, Lewis gingerly levered his fingers into the man's jacket pocket and around the wallet he'd been eyeing for the last few minutes.

At that precise moment the train jolted as it passed over a level crossing. The stranger's head tipped sideways causing his hat to slide off. Several ugly indents showed on his bald crown, surrounded by small patches of drying blood.

Lewis jumped back as if stung. He stared at the man, hardly believing his eyes; there was no doubt he was not only dead but had been murdered!

Unsure what to do, Lewis slipped out of the compartment and looked up and down the corridor. *Run for it!* a voice in his head shouted.

There was no one to his left but to his right were a young man and woman locked in an embrace. The man was engrossed in kissing his companion's neck, seemingly completely unaware of Lewis's presence.

The woman turned to face Lewis, a grin breaking out on her pretty face. Slowly she lifted one side of her petticoat, revealing a tantalising amount of bare thigh.

Lewis dragged his gaze away from her and looked out of the window. He thought about the dead man's wallet he had intended pilfering. Had he touched it? He had read in the paper recently about one Albert Stratton who had been convicted of murder on the strength of a thumbprint he had left on his victim's cash box.

Lewis came to a decision. The train was pulling in to Godalming but he yanked the communication cord anyway.

*****

Lewis spent two hours in the waiting room at Godalming station before finally he was escorted to the stationmaster's office for questioning by the police.

There were two men in the room. The first was a middle-aged gentleman who looked resplendent in a dark blue tunic with silver buttons. He was staring out of the window and gently rocking back and forth on his heels, his hands clasped behind his back. The second was seated in the far corner with a notebook and ballpoint pen. He had a ruddy complexion and large earlobes, but Lewis suspected he had barely turned twenty.

Neither man spoke for some moments which added to Lewis's discomfort. Eventually the man by the window turned abruptly and said: -

'Mr Pomfret? Please sit down. I am Inspector Adcock of Scotland Yard and this is Constable Forrester. We are here to investigate a suspicious death and I'd be obliged by your full cooperation.'

Lewis took a seat while the Inspector remained standing. He vaguely wondered whether this was some sort of ploy to put him at a disadvantage.

'Now, I believe you discovered the gentleman sitting opposite you on the train was dead, but not until you reached Godalming. How did that come about?'

'Well, Inspector,' Lewis said, trying to sound breezy and serious at the same time, 'I got on at Woking and went into a compartment that had two occupants, one being the deceased and another gentleman.'

'Can you describe the other gentleman?'

Lewis did so as far as he was able.

'Then what happened?'

'The second gentleman got off at Guildford leaving me alone with the deceased. He—the deceased, that is—was sitting quite peacefully, having forty winks I reckoned. Then, without warning, the poor feller keeled over along with his topper and straight away I realised he was a goner and someone must have bashed him on the bonce.'

'So you're saying he must have been dead before you got on the train at Woking?'

'Yeah. Well it's obvious, ain't it?'

'Is it?'

The Inspector waited but Lewis wasn't going to be drawn.

'It seems to me, Mr Pomfret, that we only have your word for it. There also seems to be no one to confirm there was another gentleman in the compartment who, according to you, got off at Guildford.'

Lewis bravely pointed a finger. 'Now look 'ere, Inspector, if someone killed the feller it weren't me, so I'm not swinging for it, see? I've told you everything exactly as it happened.'

Which wasn't strictly true, he realised. For he hadn't mentioned the dead man's wallet he had intended stealing.

'Besides,' he added, 'if it was me that topped him I would hardly 'ave alerted everyone by pulling the emergency cord, would I?'

'As I understand it,' Inspector Adcock said, with an air of menace, 'you were seen leaving the compartment just before the train reached Godalming. So rather than bring suspicion on yourself by scarpering, you pretended you'd only just discovered your fellow passenger was dead even though you'd been sitting next to him since Woking. And even if your story about another gentleman getting off at Guildford is true, you still had ample time to commit the murder.'

Lewis rubbed his forehead, trying to decide what to say next. But the Inspector had placed his hands on the table and was glaring at him.

'You were found to have £125 in your pocket. The deceased gentleman - a respectable, well-to-do chap by the looks of it - was carrying nothing except a hotel receipt and his train ticket. Now what, I ask you, should I deduce from that?'

'All I can tell you, Inspector, is that I won the brass on cards last night at my friend's place in Woking. He'll vouch for me.'

'Ah, a spot of illegal gambling! Your story seems to be getting more colourful by the minute, Mr Pomfret... Or should I call you Light-Fingered Louis, one of the most infamous thieves in the South of England?'

Lewis breathed deeply and said: 'I may have got into trouble for relieving the rich of their money occasionally but one thing I am not, Inspector, is a bleeding cold-blooded bludger!'

'Who said anything about the murder being committed in cold blood? I suggest that when you found yourself alone in the compartment with the gentleman, you decided you were going to rob him and when he fought back you killed him.'

'And what am I supposed to have killed him with?'

'Something you disposed of by throwing it out of the window, I should think. Whatever it was, rest assured we'll find it, Mr Pomfret.'

38

'If you do, check it for fingerprints; that's the new thing with you lot, ain't it? 'Cause you won't find no prints of mine on it.'

Inspector Adcock stroked his whiskers thoughtfully. Still glaring at Lewis, he said: 'Isn't it normally the suspect with opportunity and motive that is revealed as the murderer, Constable Forrester?'

'Certainly in my experience, sir.'

Lewis almost laughed. Surely the lad was far too wet behind those huge earlobes to have brought any arch villains to justice.

Happily, the inspector's next words spelled an end to Lewis's ordeal, at least for the moment. 'Right, Mr Pomfret, you're free to go. That is, once you have provided my colleague with your fingerprints—which I take it you've no objection to? And with your home address and that of your friend in Woking, of course.'

Lewis was tempted to say they probably had a record of his address already, but thought better of it.

*****

On collecting his belongings Lewis was relieved to find all his money intact. Perhaps, he thought, the police took the view he hadn't stolen from the dead man after all. But a murder charge remained a dreadful possibility.

By this time, he was both hungry and thirsty. Rather than catch the next train home he decided to try one of Godalming's hostelries, The Star in Church Street. He ordered pie and mash and a tankard of ale and settled down to read the early edition of the Evening Standard he had bought outside the station. The front page held brief details about a man who had died in 'suspicious circumstances' on that morning's 9.09 from Waterloo to Portsmouth, followed by an urgent appeal for anyone travelling on the same train to contact the police immediately in case they had information that might assist with the investigation.

After browsing through the rest of the paper, which contained little that interested him, Lewis peered round the pub to observe the other punters. News of the murder had clearly filtered through as most people seemed to be discussing it in an excitable manner. Lewis's presence was barely noticed however; he was in no doubt nobody else in the pub was aware of his involvement.

Once Lewis had finished his meal and was about to set off for home, a man carrying a golf bag strode into the pub and said at large: 'Anyone fancy a round?'

'If you're buying!' a wag at the bar replied.

The simple joke was lost on Lewis who was staring at the golf bag, deep in thought. Inspector Adcock had suggested the murderer had thrown the murder weapon - whatever it was - out of the window. But what if they hadn't? What if they'd had a bag of some description and had simply put the weapon in it once satisfied the victim was dead?

In his mind's eye Lewis pictured the snuff-taking gentleman who had been in the same compartment and had alighted at Guildford. Hadn't he carried a briefcase with him?

Lewis tried to imagine the man committing the murder when he and the victim had been alone together. But why hadn't he then fled the scene? Perhaps he, like Lewis, had been a complete innocent and had assumed the other occupant was simply asleep.

Then Lewis had another thought. One that set his pulse racing.

*****

On returning to Godalming station Lewis was informed that Inspector Adcock and Constable Forrester had left a little while ago. However, the stationmaster directed Lewis to the local nick and on arriving there was told the detectives were interviewing a member of the public and would Mr Pomfret mind waiting?

Presently Lewis heard a door open and the deep voice of Inspector Adcock thanking a Mr Jones for coming forward so promptly. When the visitor came into view Lewis was surprised to see that it was the snuff-taking gentleman who had shared the compartment with himself and the deceased and had alighted at Guildford.

'Ah, Mr Pomfret,' the inspector said as Mr Jones took his leave. 'I thought you'd be back in Pompey by now. Come through, will you?'

Lewis was led to a windowless room which comprised only a table and chairs. Mindful of his uncomfortable interview with the inspector earlier, Lewis remained standing. 'Firstly,' he said, 'that gentleman who just left - Jones, I think you called 'im - was the one in the same compartment as me this morning.'

'Yes, I'm aware of that,' the Inspector replied.

'Did he back up my story then?'

The detective grimaced. 'I'm not obliged to satisfy your curiosity on any particular matter, Mr Pomfret. All I would say is that Mr Jones has been able to assist us with our enquiries.'

'Good,' Lewis said. 'Because I reckon the murder took place before Mr Jones got on the train. Just like me, he thought the chap in the topper was fast asleep when in fact he was already dead. I'm right, aren't I?'

The Inspector didn't reply but instead said: 'Is there a reason you've come to see me this afternoon, apart from having a chinwag about this morning's events?'

'Do I get a reward if I provide information that leads to the arrest of the murderer?'

'*Reward?*' the inspector bellowed, taking Lewis by surprise. 'If you have important information, sonny, you better let me have it right now. Otherwise you'll be behind bars before you can say Jack Robinson!'

Lewis shifted nervously. 'I suppose it's more of a hunch than information.'

A subtle change passed over the detective's face. 'This had better be good,' he whispered.

Somewhat hesitantly Lewis outlined his theory.

*****

A few days later over breakfast Lewis read with interest the headline news in the Daily Telegraph:

WOMAN CHARGED IN SURREY RAILWAY MURDER CASE

'Alice Gilchrist, a 42-year-old spinster from Woking, has been charged with the unlawful murder of Ronald Stephens, 53, also of Woking, on the morning of 6th June. It is understood Miss Gilchrist and Mr Stephens were travelling on a Portsmouth-bound train from Waterloo when the crime is alleged to have taken place. In a statement Inspector George Adcock of Scotland Yard reported that Miss Gilchrist and Mr Stephens had played in a concert the previous evening at the Royal Albert Hall before spending the night in rooms at the Hyde Park Hotel. On the journey home a row is said to have broken out regarding the money due to Miss Gilchrist from the concert. Miss Gilchrist, the percussionist in the band, is alleged to have bludgeoned Mr Stephens to death while he slept following their row, using a tubular bell mallet which was later discovered by police in a music case at her home address in Woking. She is also alleged to have stolen Mr Stephens' money following the murder.

'The trial is due to take place at The Old Bailey today.'

Lewis put down the paper and gazed out of the window.

He recalled the anxiety etched across Alice Gilchrist's face as he had helped with her cases at Woking station. She had given him a quizzical look at the time and now he understood why. He vaguely wondered what conclusion Inspector Adcock would have drawn had he found Lewis's fingerprints on the bag that had contained the murder weapon!

He also remembered thinking what a petite lady Alice Gilchrist was. Incredible to think she had been the perpetrator of such a heinous crime.

Lewis pondered over the chain of events leading to her arrest. He recalled from his initial interview with Inspector Adcock that the detective had mentioned finding a hotel receipt on the corpse. No doubt the inspector would have contacted the hotel manager who perhaps had held a record of Alice's home address as she also had stayed the night at the hotel. Or maybe he had tracked her down through the band in which both she and the deceased had performed the previous evening. Or was it the case that Mr Jones, the venerable snuff-taking gentleman, had witnessed her leaving the compartment in which the murder had taken place?

He suspected he would never know the answers to these questions. But at least he'd not been charged with anything and could take satisfaction from having been instrumental - he chuckled at his own joke - in bringing the murderer of Ronald Stephens to justice.

Godalming Events

Victorian 1837 – 1861
1861 – Godalming Public Hall opened in Bridge Street.
1859 – Godalming Railway Station opened and railway extended from Godalming to Portsmouth.
1849 – London and South Western Railway extended from Guildford to Godalming (old station on corner of Meadrow and Chalk Road).
1843 – Godalming National School moved from the Mint Street to Moss Lane.
1837 – Gas Works established at the Wharf.

'WRONG MEDICAL CARD' OR 'INCIDENT ON FLAMBARD WAY'

Poem by Christine Butler

'That's not me, it's not my card,' he said. They couldn't hear.

What luck to find a wallet, but the car had been too near.

Now they thought he needed treatment that might kill him.

He lay there helpless on the bed.

'Oh, listen please… or I might soon be dead.'

Godalming Events

Third Millennium 2000 – Today
2017 – Great Godalming Duck Race held in the park.
2017 – Godalming Tales published.
2018 – Godalming Tales Vol. 2 published.
2008 - GOLO first independent town society lottery started.
2005 - Music in the Park Concerts commenced.

NO REFUNDS

by Louise Honeysett

'Oh God', I thought, as I jerked into consciousness, furry tongued and head starting to bang. 'What happened last night?'

I rolled over, the banging worsening to a stabbing pain in my temple. Scared to move again for fear of further developments, I tried to think back to the previous evening's events. I'd gone out for the first time in weeks - well, months really, if I'm being honest. Party invitations hadn't exactly been flooding in of late, so when Jonno - an old friend from Godalming College - had texted about his 30th birthday bash at the newly reopened Cinderella's club in Guildford I'd jumped at the chance to get out and live a little.

In retrospect I might have overcompensated a bit with the drinks, a fact hard to escape with this hangover from hell looming. I lay for a while, tangled in sweaty sheets, remembering random chats with old school friends, shouted over the cheesy music of the club. Snatches of bad dancing came back, quite a lot of queueing at the bar…I groaned at the memory of a sneaky cigarette out back; I'd given up months ago and was annoyed at myself for the lapse.

But overall, nothing too worrying came to mind. Admittedly there were a few blanks and I couldn't remember getting home - but clearly I did,

47

so I assumed the night had ended with the usual stumble into a cab.

Somewhat buoyed by this conclusion, I forced myself to get up and into the bathroom. Teeth brushed, hot shower taken, I started to feel slightly more human, although my head was still thumping.

That's when the text message arrived. Unknown number.

'I've got some for you, but it wasn't easy. You owe me.'

I read the message twice more, trying to connect it to the mists of last night's memories. Nothing. Heart starting to beat a little quicker, I scrolled up and saw two other messages from the same sender, both sent in the small hours of the morning.

The first said: 'Was surprised to see you, didn't think you came here anymore after what happened last year.

Anyway, I'll see what I can do but can't make any promises'

The second: 'Harold won't be happy about this, mind!'

As I worked through my mental rolodex looking for Harolds, my heart really started to race. Only one came to mind, and he wasn't someone I wanted to text me. I slowly poured myself a cup of strong coffee and turned on the telly, trying desperately to recall another Harold, but my mind kept going returning to Harry Brown.

I'd met Harry a year before, not long after my Dad's funeral. Dad's death by heart attack had come out of nowhere and taken us all by surprise. His daily jogs around the neighbourhood were a family joke, his health generally excellent - we never thought he'd be taken from us so soon. I'd struggled a lot with his loss, not just the empty seat at the table and the thought that I'd never hear his voice again, but also being forced to consider my own mortality. If Dad could go young, why not me? And what had I achieved so far in my life?

It was a dark time, and although at first I tried to drown out these thoughts through long, rowdy nights down the pub every night of the week, after a while the invites started drying up. Looking back, I can see that the casual acquaintances and work colleagues I'd been drinking with simply weren't willing to take on the burden of a clearly depressed almost-stranger, and I can't blame them for it. But at the time the rejection was a major blow and pushed me further into the dark.

Harry was a friend of a friend of a friend, and I knew he had drug connections. I'm ashamed to admit I sought him out, and before long was a regular customer, buying from him or whichever of his circle I could find, not that he was happy when the money was in someone else's pocket.

For several months I lurked in the shadows of drug use, somehow dragging myself out of bed to go to work every day, but never fully hiding my problems from anyone who cared enough to notice. The wake-up call came when my manager pulled me to one side and gave me a brochure for the employee assistance programme. He didn't say much, but gave me a stern look that spoke volumes. The grief counselling I received chipped away at the darkness, and eventually I started to see the light again. My relationship with Harry ended with a big argument and a final payment on my part for alleged 'outstanding debts'. I had avoided him ever since.

Or so I thought. I scrambled over last night's timeline again, trying to see how Harry and his gang might fit in, urgently hoping they didn't. Nothing new came back, but it occurred to me that I hadn't been alone. I pinged a message over to Jonno, trying to subtly find out if he knew more. Then I slumped on the sofa, breathing deeply to try and slow my racing heart.

Finally, Jonno replied.

'Good night last night, thx for coming! You seemed like you were having fun, lost track of you for a while but when I saw you again you were grinning from ear to ear and dancing like a loon. Man am I suffering today lol. Fry up here I come'

My stomach lurched as I flashed back to a year ago, where long nights of dilated pupils and unbounding energy were inevitably followed by energy crashes and a head full of fog and regret. I tried to remember if that was how I'd felt this morning. I didn't think it had been anything more than your bog-standard booze hangover, but the more I dwelt on it the more I had a sinking feeling that it had been more. Had I fallen into that hole again, and had I made plans to fall even further?

A new text message from the unknown number interrupted my thoughts:

'Are you getting these messages?

Don't leave me hanging, mate!

When can we meet so I can hand over the goods?'

Panic kicked in, and I couldn't help but hear the words in Harry's threatening tones. My only thought was to extract myself from this situation as quickly as possible, so for the first time I sent a reply:

'Sorry, I've changed my mind, I don't want it anymore'

I sat staring at my phone for what felt like hours, hoping that was the end of that. But the response came through:

'What do you mean?! You can't pull out now, you already paid me, you tit!'

Alarm spread through me on reading these words. I quickly pulled up my banking app, and to my horror saw a cash withdrawal the previous night, for £150. My heart sank. It was clear now – I must have bumped into one of Harry's friends in the club, and they'd convinced me to buy pills, one for now, more for later. I couldn't remember it at all, but resigned myself to the unavoidable truth.

The money was a real blow – I had been planning to buy a new phone for a while, just waiting for a good deal. I would have to wait months longer now. The frustration I felt was enough to spur me to action. I grabbed my phone, and typed out another reply:

'OK fine, I'll meet you at Guildford bus station in half an hour.'

As I jumped on the bus, I practised my speech in my head. Drug dealers weren't exactly known for their benevolence, but maybe if I made a compelling case he might give me back my money without any pills changing hands? It was worth a try.

Arriving at the bus station, heart pounding, I looked around, hoping to recognise one of Harry's friends. Nobody stood out so I lingered for a while scanning the crowd. 15 minutes passed, with most people disappearing off onto buses. One man was left; middle aged in a blazer and loafers. He didn't look much like one of Harry's lot, but then who's to say drug dealers can't have style? I watched him pull out his phone and type, and immediately a text pinged on my phone:

'You coming or what??'

Taking a deep breath, a lump in my throat, I walked over and tapped him on the shoulder.

*****

I sat at the front of the bus, looking out at the sun struggling to break through the clouds. The absurdity of what had just happened left me reeling. I thought about Roger, the man at the bus stop. I thought about his friend Jeremy, who had a phone number one digit different to mine, and Jeremy's plan to buy a birthday present for his sister Anne. Anne loved a particular vintage of wine, but her husband Harold wasn't a fan, said it was a waste of money. So, Jeremy plotted with Roger to buy some for her as a surprise. Roger was a little taken aback when Jeremy seemed to have forgotten about this plan, but had to laugh when we met and the pieces of the puzzle clicked into place.

Opening my front door and kicking off my shoes, I felt like a total prat. What a load of stress over nothing! Safe from Harry's grip once more, with the hangover finally subsiding, I settled onto the sofa, but something sharp poked into my back. Reaching round I pulled out a plastic bag with a box inside. What else could it be but a new phone, the model I'd had my eye on, with a receipt for £150 stamped the night before.

I wouldn't be forgetting that purchase again in a hurry!

GRAVEYARD

by David Lowther

John strode jauntily through the entrance of The King's Arms Hotel in Godalming High Street.

'Mr Wilson?' asked the girl on reception, a brunette in, John guessed, her late teens.

'It is,' came the reply. 'I hope I'm not too late for dinner.'

'Of course not, sir. Just fill in the register and you'll have time to settle in to your room and have a wash before you eat. Here's your key. It's room 7 on the first floor.'

'Thank you. Did you get my message about the bicycle?'

'We did. It'll be ready for you first thing in the morning.'

'Thank you,' said John who picked up his rather heavy looking suitcase and began to climb the staircase.

'What a nice man,' thought Judy as she watched him depart.

'A bit of alright that,' thought John. 'Could be OK there.'

John let himself into the room, threw his case on to the bed, took off his jacket and had a quick wash. He dried himself then, noticing that the wardrobe had a lock, secured the case in there. Then it was jacket on and downstairs for dinner. Passing reception, he gave Judy a beaming smile and received a slightly less enthusiastic one in response. Dinner was passable with brown Windsor soup followed by breaded place and chips and finished off with rhubarb crumble and custard and a cup of coffee.

It was late September 1942 and the weather had been fine. It was dark outside but by no means cold and John felt that he had chosen the right time to take a short cycling break. His journey from London Waterloo to Godalming had been uneventful except that the train had been on time and wasn't crowded, both unusual occurrences in wartime England. He downed a pint of watered-down beer and then made for his room. Lying on the bed, he spread out a local map and studied it intensely for half an hour. He jotted down a few notes then got undressed, brushed his teeth and climbed under the sheets. The latest Agatha Christie novel, The Body in the Library, kept him awake for another twenty minutes and then he drifted off into a dreamless sleep.

Bacon, eggs, tomato and fried bread was just the kind of start to the day John needed before his bike ride. But he wasn't going to get it. Spam and baked beans were the best the Kings Arms could manage from their rations, despite coming up with a decent dinner the evening before. Another fine day with hardly a cloud in the sky more than made up for the privations of rationing and, suitably dressed in fawn casual trousers and a thin blue jumper over a white open necked shirt, he stepped into the back yard of the hotel where his bicycle awaited him. He expected to be back in time for lunch so didn't bother with sandwiches. With a smile on his face, this pleasant young man set off down Bridge Street, crossed the Town Bridge and peddled towards Guildford.

Leaving the Guildford Road, John turned left towards Farnham and then pedalled energetically through Compton passing acres of woodland on either side of the road which was largely flat. Puttenham was the next village and the road dropped sharply towards Wanborough.

Vera was taking advantage of the fine weather to smoke a cigarette at the gate to the entrance to Wanborough Manor. Dashing down from London for a quick visit, she needed a short break before she went indoors to tackle the day's tasks. Wearing a dark green twin set, brown tweed skirt and sensible brown shoes, she appeared to be in her thirties. Fair haired, she had business-like features and she looked as if she could handle herself in a wartime world of men. Suddenly, she became aware of a cyclist approaching. A very dark-haired young man with an open pleasant face pulled up alongside her. He too seemed to be in his thirties and was, as far as she could judge, tall and athletic looking.

'Good morning,' the young man said.

'And good morning to you, 'Vera replied. 'It's a beautiful day.'

'It certainly is.'

'Do you live around here or are you on holiday?' Vera asked.

'I work in London. Thought I'd take a couple of days to do some cycling.'

'Very wise. You never know when the chance might come again. I presume you're usually in uniform?'

'Of course. I'm in the RAF but more than that I can't tell you. What about you. Do you live around here?'

'Yes. I work in the Manor,' she said pointing towards the large house. 'I'm just a clerk.'

'What goes on in there?'

'I've no real idea but then I wouldn't tell you if I knew, just as I wouldn't expect you to tell me what your duties were in the RAF.'

John laughed. 'You're quite right. I must be off. Got to get to The King's Arms in Godalming in time for lunch.'

'I know it,' Vera replied. 'Very nice. You're staying there?

'Just for a couple of nights. Must be off. Goodbye.'

'Goodbye young man.'

'Harmless spinster,' thought John, as he began the return journey.

As soon as John was out of sight, Vera went through the gate to the Manor, stepped smartly though the front door, turned left and pushed open the heavy oak door that took her into a busy office.

'Telephone line to London, now,' she snapped.

'Yes ma'am.'

John made it back to Godalming with a little difficulty. Uphill seemed more frequent than downhill on the return trip but, he reasoned to himself, it must have been the other way round on the way out. So, it was with a little relief that he finally reached The King's Arms, ready to enjoy a pleasant lunch. Following this, rest seemed to be in order so he went to his room and lay down on his bed for an hour. Time to chat up Judy, he thought so he made his way downstairs where, to his huge disappointment, he found a rather stone-faced matron manning reception. He smiled a 'good afternoon' then set off to explore the town.

Godalming High Street looked a real treat with crowds thronging the multitude of shops with many of the citizens wishing him a cheerful 'good afternoon.' Belatedly he bought a morning paper and took it back to the hotel where he caught up with the war news over a pot of tea. Hard news was thin on the ground. Anthony Eden, the Foreign Secretary had made a speech in Leamington Spa about not very much in particular and a Soviet counter-attack had begun near Stalingrad. While he was lazily drifting through the newspaper and mentally planning what he would do the next day, he spotted a black Ford

Anglia draw into the car park at the rear of the hotel. A stunning blonde got out, grabbed a large suitcase from the boot and made her way to the front of the hotel via the alley at the side.

'I'm Margaret Rhodes,' the young girl announced to the receptionist.

'Oh yes Miss Rhodes. We got your telegram. We've booked you in for three nights. Is that correct?'

'Thank you. That's fine.'

'Room 9 on the first floor,' the receptionist said, handing Margaret the key.

'Thank you. I'll be down for dinner. Is 6.30 OK?'

'Certainly Miss Rhodes.'

Margaret made her way to her room and lay on the bed for a rest before dinner and thought to what lay ahead.

John meanwhile was still downstairs and was looking forward to his dinner and not just because he knew he'd be hungry before too long. Surely, the gorgeous woman he'd seen arriving half an hour ago would be coming down to dinner. A great chance to make her acquaintance beckoned. Thank heavens for that. Something to look forward to in this dreary town.

Margaret was already sitting at her table when John arrived in the dining room. He looked at her and she paused from sipping her soup to give him a dazzling smile. While he was enjoying his meal, John studied the girl. She was blue eyed and her blonde hair was meticulously waved at the top and tumbled down to her shoulders in curls. She was wearing a French navy-blue plain dress and, as far as he could see, had a fine pair of legs. Certainly, her ankles were very attractive.

Frequent smiles were exchanged between the two tables so it appeared only natural that, their meals completed, they should make their way to the bar and sit together. Introductions were made and Margaret sat in the corner of the bar area while John fetched the drinks; tonic for the lady and another watery pint for him.

'What brings you to Godalming?' John asked.

'Just a few days away from the stress of London,' she replied. 'I'd heard that Godalming was a fine centre for motor touring and, because I work in the Admiralty, I was able to cadge a few extra petrol coupons from my boss who said I'd been working too hard and deserved a break. And you?'

'Just a couple of days leave from the RAF. I'm stationed near London. I don't have a car but the hotel has loaned me a bicycle,'

'How very energetic,' Margaret laughed. 'Is London your home?'

'No York. Do you know it?'

'Not well but I did spend a week there with my parents when I was in my teens. It's a lovely place.'

'And where's your home?'

'Kingston in Surrey. I get home as often as I can but I work long hours so live in a house in Bloomsbury with some other girls. Tell me about York.'

'It's a famous Roman city and has plenty of Viking history as well. It's very flat and therefore comfortable to walk round. Some of the buildings date back centuries. The Shambles is one of the oldest streets in Europe and a stroll up there brings you to the magnificent York Minster, the city's cathedral. Oh, and they make chocolate there.'

'I remember reading about a particularly nasty air raid back in the spring. Was there much damage?' asked Margaret.

'Not a lot. I say. It's a lovely evening. Shall we go for a stroll?'

'Yes, why not? You can show me some of the sights of Godalming.'

'Right oh.' I'll just pop up to my room and replace this jacket with a sweater.'

'I'll wait for you here.'

Darkness was falling as they stepped out of the hotel into Godalming High Street. Margaret's bag was slung over her shoulder. There was little or no traffic although they did see an olive-green Post Office van at the top of the High Street. The Pepperpot came into view, a handsome two storey white building with a short clock tower on top.

'What's that?' asked Margaret.

'I asked about that when I was out walking this afternoon. It's the Town Hall, or used to be,' replied John.

'It's a very striking building. Let's see what's down here,' Margaret suggested, seizing John's hand.

John's heart was beginning to beat faster than usual and he needed no second invitation to walk down Church Street with this beautiful girl.

'The station is just down there, beyond the church,' John pointed out as they passed an ancient looking pub called The Star.

The impressive steeple of the Godalming Church loomed out of the darkness as Margaret squeezed John's hand as she led him down a path beside the church's graveyard. She slipped her left arm around his waist and looked him in the eyes.

'You're really a very nice man,' Margaret whispered, as the pair of them leant back against the graveyard wall.

'You're rather beautiful Margaret,' John breathed as he leant towards her in anticipation of a kiss, not noticing that Margaret had flicked open the catch on the front of her bag and reached inside.

'Did you not know that the Minster in York is at the top of Stonegate not the Shambles John, or is it Johann or Jan or Jens?'

Before he had a chance to reply, John felt a searing pain in his right side as Margaret slid a lethally sharpened knitting needle into his body underneath his right armpit. John's eyes bulged and his mouth flew open but no sound came out.

'It won't take long,' Margaret coolly told him. I've punctured your vital organs. You'll be dead in 5 minutes.'

John slumped to the ground, accompanied by a soft moan. Margaret stuck two fingers in her mouth and, in a most unladylike fashion, let out a piercing whistle. Two men immediately appeared from the direction of Church Street, each wearing Post Office overalls. One gave Margaret a thin dark blue sweater which she immediately put on. Then, reaching into John's trouser pocket, she took out his hotel keys.

'Where's the weapon?' one of the men asked.

'Still in him,' Margaret replied. 'Leave it in. It'll plug the hole and stop the bleeding.'

The men nodded and lifted the now lifeless body.

'Meet me in the car park at the back of the hotel,' Margaret ordered as she set up towards Church Street.

Margaret walked briskly back to The King's Arms. As she walked into the main entrance, Judy the receptionist called out.

'Miss Rhodes. I've had a telephone call for you from your sister. Your mother's been taken ill. You're to return home immediately.'

A look of concern spread over her face.

'Oh dear, I'm afraid I'll have to leave you. I'm so sorry. Can I pay for my room?'

'Just the dinner Miss Rhodes. Two and six.'

'Thank you. I'll go and get my stuff.'

Margaret ran up the stairs, let herself into her room, picked up her suitcase and lay it open on the bed. It was empty. She slipped her shoes off and silently made her way to John's room. Letting herself in with the keys she'd taken from the dying man's pockets, she scanned the room. His toiletries were by the sink and a medium sized suitcase was propped against the wardrobe. She lay it on the bed, opened and swept all of his possessions into it. This included two Agatha Christie novels which may have proved significant to the code breakers. She opened the wardrobe and was not surprised to find some note pads, a camera and a short-wave radio. Joining John's other stuff in the suitcase, she threw the wardrobe contents in, closed the lid, fastened the lock and made her way back into her own room where John's suitcase fitted nicely into her own.

'Thank you, Miss Rhodes,' Judy said as Margaret passed reception on her way out. Have you far to go?

'Kingston,' an anxious Margaret replied.

'Not far then. Safe journey and I hope you find your mother is recovering.

'Thank you.'

The look of anxiety on Margaret's face was replaced by a smile of satisfaction as she passed the suitcase to the Post Office men.

'Straight to Baker Street,' Margaret ordered. 'Miss Atkins will tell you what to dispose of. She'll keep the rest.

'Yes ma'am.'

'And thank you and well done,' Margaret told them.

A nod from one of the men and they climbed into the van and were away. Margaret stepped into the Anglia and set off.

'Vera will be pleased with me,' she said to herself.

FOOTNOTE

Wanborough Manor served as Special Training School 5 of the Special Operations Executive (SOE) during the Second World War.

Vera Atkins CBE was Assistant to Section Head Maurice Buckmaster in the SOE.

EGGS BENEDICT

by Paul Rennie

Benedict Ainsworth was an Oologist, a collector of birds' eggs. But this was a bit of a misnomer. Rather than being a Research Scientist who had specialised in this branch of Ornithology after years of academia, Benedict was merely a common egg thief, who had single-handedly brought many rare species of British wild birds close to extinction by his indiscriminate pillaging of their nests. His obsession started in his teens as he slowly built up one of the largest illegal collections of bird eggs in the country. In his house, garage and sheds were cabinets and drawers filled with carefully labelled and catalogued eggs, each resting in a cocoon of cotton wool. By 2018, he was a slightly overweight middle-aged loner, with long greasy greying hair and beard, permanently dressed in grubby khaki strung with binoculars. He had managed to collect one or more eggs of almost every British species of wild bird, including very rare ones such as Ospreys and Montagu's Harriers, travelling the country and often taking huge risks to obtain them. Unfortunately, such a large, valuable and definitely illegal collection would have attracted the attention of the authorities and a long prison sentence, so he had to keep his triumphs to himself. Nobody knew about his collection, except for a few like-minded collectors who shared his obsession and conducted illicit trading with him on the dark web.

His was undoubtedly the largest and most extensive collection amongst his peers, and, for this reason, his soubriquet became '*Eggs Benedict*'.

*****

In March 2018, the town of Godalming in Surrey received the highly unusual visit of a pair of Red Footed Falcons. Their usual range was East Europe, but this pair on their migratory travels, spotted something they liked about Busbridge and decided to make it their home for the breeding season. There had been previous sightings of solitary migratory birds in the UK, but never in this area. This pair had come a long way from their usual range in Kazakhstan, not a place that one would expect to have much in common with the Surrey Hills, but maybe the Falcons noticed a passing resemblance to the lush hills and valleys of Tian Shan, and liked what they saw. More likely, though, is that they saw an opportunity in the high-end housing market, having spotted a Rookery in a large Sweet Chestnut tree in a field near Tuesley Lane.

Now, if there is one thing Red Footed Falcons like, it's a Rook's nest. Characteristically built high up in trees to catch the wind and safe from predators, these sturdy ready-made twiggy constructions were just what our Falcon pair needed. It didn't matter that the nest was already occupied by its owners, Falcons being birds of prey, and two together, were more than enough to evict the tenants. They moved into a nicely positioned nest on the outskirts of Rook village. Ok, there was a lot of squawking and cawing by the whole Rookery, but you get that anyway with Rooks squabbling amongst themselves. After a few tentative attempts at mobbing the squatters to move them on, the Rooks decided that their chicks probably wouldn't be safe living next door to a family that would probably eat them, and moved en masse to a new location. The Falcons then moved upmarket to the newly vacated penthouse apartment and settled down to do what breeding pairs do. This was unusual in its own right, because Red Footed Falcons normally like to live in colonies. This pair seemed quite happy with their own company, or maybe they had some pioneering spirit, the avian equivalent of colonizing Mars.

As you can imagine, such an unprecedented visit to sleepy Godalming caused quite a stir. It was unheard of, and not just a fleeting visit like that of Peter the Great (the story of which Godalming has dined out on for nearly four centuries). No, these exotic visitors had made their home in the town. Bird watchers and twitchers descended on Busbridge in their droves, armed with telescopes, binoculars and huge telephoto lenses, trampling through fields and gardens hoping to catch a glimpse of such a rare occurrence. The townsfolk were more entertained by sightings of these camouflage-clad beings than by the birds themselves, which were relatively small and dull bluish grey, apart from their red legs and feet. The female had a slightly more interesting orange head and white face, but since she left the nest only rarely, was not seen very often. The spotters were rewarded with rather a similar lack of activity. The

Falcons occasionally flew off in search of a snack, but most of the time they seemed happy sitting in their love nest, hidden from direct view by the height of the tree, and the twigs and foliage around them. A remote camera was carefully installed and this revealed that the female had laid three brick red eggs and the birds were taking it in turns to incubate them.

Benedict through his connections already knew this. In his cabinet there was an empty space that he had been hoping for years to fill with a Red Footed Falcon egg or two. He coveted these things of beauty, and, with such a distinctive colour they would stand out amongst the predominantly pastel shades of most of his collection. He had to get his hands on them. It would be the pinnacle of his life's work, Eldorado, the Holy Grail, the Rosetta stone. It would be a difficult mission and would require careful planning to avoid being caught and prosecuted, but he had done this before. The arrivals had attracted huge attention from the media, not to mention sightseers, and the remote camera footage was linked to Spring Watch so that the whole country could see the nest live on the BBC. A challenge indeed, but a risk he was prepared to take. He had to move quickly, though, otherwise the eggs would hatch and be of no use to him. He had already staked out the nesting site, having already made the long drive to Surrey from Cannock where he lived. Once there he had mingled with the bird spotters staked out in the nearby fields. He was not really interested in the Falcons themselves, he wanted their valuable eggs, and it didn't matter to him if he ruined such a unique spectacle in the process. He spent the day working out angles and routes up the tree. It was going to be tough, but he decided it would be possible under the cover of darkness. He drove back home to wait for the initial interest to die down.

*****

Over the next few days, he studied the live feed on the BBC waiting for the right moment. His first move was to create fake eggs to replace the real ones in the nest. Using modelling clay, he fashioned three eggs of the right size and shape, and then painted them carefully with acrylic paints to look like the real thing. When finished he held them up and admired them. They were things of beauty, perfect shiny red speckled ovoids, but only the real ones would do for him. When the next moonless night came round, he tucked the fake eggs into his rucksack, with his climbing equipment, and infra-red light, and set off again on the drive south. On the A34, he stopped at one of those roadside vans, and bought himself a round of his favourite egg mayonnaise sandwiches, the irony of the purchase completely lost on him. It was the end of a long hot day, and the van owner was just about to close up. The sandwiches had been sitting around and looked a bit curled up, but Benedict was no gourmet, and had seen worse. He ate one immediately with a cup of coffee, and kept the other for his vigil.

He finally reached a layby near the nesting site, and changed into his black clothing, leaving off his balaclava for the time being. It was 1am, and he had to wait for a couple of hours to make sure there weren't any nosy twitchers around to see him. He opened a flask of tea and finished the egg sandwiches. Now we will never know how the *Salmonella enterica* got into the sandwiches. It could have come from the eggs themselves, but equally it could have been the mayonnaise, which, if made traditionally, would have contained raw egg, or it might have been the slightly insanitary conditions and lack of handwashing facilities in the roadside van. Whichever, there was a particularly nasty variant of the bacterium in the sandwiches, and once in Benedict's stomach, the newly liberated enterotoxin got to work on his digestive system. He burped slightly and felt a bit queasy, but he put it down to nerves at what he was about to undertake.

At 3am he was ready to make his move, and pulled the balaclava over his head and applied some camouflage paint to his face as a final touch. He climbed over a fence and walked across the field towards the Chestnut tree. Excellent, it was a pitch-black night with no moonlight, so he turned on his infrared night sight. He could see the tree clearly, and there was nobody around. At the base he could see the wire running up the trunk that was connected to the remote camera. He would deal with that later as he didn't want to alert any viewers yet. His stomach gurgled and he felt a slight dizziness, easily confused with the excitement and anticipation of his quarry. The tree was enormous, but he knew that already after studying the BBC footage, and he knew the nest was about 80 feet from the ground, but at least there were plenty of branches leading up to it.

He'd climbed higher and harder trees than this when raiding eagles' nests in Scotland. He placed a small extending ladder against the trunk, and then after climbing it, he threw a rope around the lowest branch and using a harness and ratchet system, hauled himself up, scrabbling his feet against the rough bark. His head swam and he felt hot, but with a cold sweat on his face. The hardest bit was over. From here on up the branches were spaced nicely to reach his goal. He could just see a tiny red light on the camera, and noted the direction it was facing. He climbed up to the next level of branches and paused to catch his breath. The Salmonella in his system had multiplied a bit, and more of the enterotoxin entered his bloodstream. He was feeling distinctly unwell, but he was not giving up now he had got so far.

He climbed to the next level, and now he could see about 10 feet above him the two Falcons sitting on the nest, their warm bodies and especially their eyes glowing in the infrared light as they watched him suspiciously. He moved closer, and the birds made their characteristic '*ke*' warning call, which may have been a Kazakhstani swear word, hopped off the nest and shuffled along a nearby branch glaring at him. Perfect, he could now see the eggs and the camera wouldn't pick up that something was wrong. He worked his way up and round so that he was behind the camera, and found where the lead was plugged into it. Careful not to shake the camera too much, he carefully unscrewed and pulled off the lead.

He knew that the remote feed would go blank, so his intention was to swap the eggs quickly, refit the lead, and hope that the temporary break in transmission would be assumed to be a glitch. The nest was a bit of a stretch, and the Rooks had built it to be well defended. He had another bout of dizziness and nausea, but not long now.

He straddled the branch that the nest was on and slithered commando fashion towards the nest. As he went, he pulled the fake eggs out of a pouch on his jacket in readiness. He reached towards the nest. Nearly there. He shuffled a bit further and, as his fingertips felt the smooth warmth of the first egg, his stomach heaved, his vision closed in, all went black, and he passed out. His unconscious body rotated round the tree branch until he was hanging beneath it by his legs and arm like a sloth, and then, as his muscles relaxed, he fell crashing through the foliage and hit the ground with a thud. The Falcons looked down, then at each other, shrugged their wings, and hopped back onto the nest

At first light a crew of technicians arrived to sort out the remote camera that had gone on the blink during the night. They first spotted the ladder against the tree trunk, and then around the back they found a figure dressed in black from head to toe. They could tell that things weren't right from the strange positions of his arms and legs. It looked like an unnaturally twisted Action Man doll. They called the emergency services and Benedict was taken by ambulance to the Royal Surrey Hospital and admitted with multiple fractures. It was a week later that he recovered consciousness. He had broken both arms and both legs, and it was assumed that he had somehow survived what should have been a fatal drop, because he had bounced off all of the branches on the way down. As it was, he was strapped up in plaster casts on his legs and arms, just like in those hospital comedy programmes. A nurse entered the room and looked at him.

'Hello Benedict, how are you feeling? You've had a nasty fall and broken a few things, so it's going to be a bit sore and you're going to be here for some time. You've had some visitors and some more bad news, there's a policeman outside that would like a word with you. It seems they have visited your house in Cannock and found some interesting things. But before that, you ought to have something to eat, and I'll have to feed you because you can't use your arms. I've got some nice scrambled egg for you, so open wide.'

In the corner of the room, through the slit in the bandages on his face, Benedict could see a TV screen and the image of a bird nest. He could just catch Chris Packham's excited voice telling Springwatch viewers that the first Red Footed Falcon egg was just starting to hatch.

THE ELECTRIC CAR

by Ian Honeysett

I've always been interested – nay, fascinated – by innovation. I'm what they call an early- adopter. Ahead of the pack. Back in 1975 when I was growing up in Godalming, I persuaded my dad to buy a Betamax video recorder. Not cheap but I somehow knew it would take off. 10 years later, I spent all my savings on a Sinclair C5 – a revolutionary electric vehicle which cost £399 – a bargain. Sad that only 500 sold and that it was voted the greatest innovation disaster of all time. But I can tell you, there was nothing quite like zipping along at 15 mph. Until you reached a hill of course, but then it was early days.

Anyway, when electric cars were advertised, I determined that I should get one. Unfortunately, I had never actually learned to drive so I wasn't a very early adopter in this case. But today, having just passed my driving test, I finally did it and bought one. I'd found a dealer in the Midlands who was selling them at a very good price so I took the train up there and am now driving this little beauty back home to Godalming. And it's so smooth. I checked that I could do the journey on just one charge and he assured me I probably could. Provided I didn't drive too fast! But, given my lack of motoring experience, that isn't a problem although he warned me that the car can go very fast. As I soon discovered when I almost hit 60. So here I am, zipping along (shades of the Sinclair C5) the A-something or other as I thought it best to avoid motorways in case other drivers weren't too happy at me doing, what, 43 mph. Some people are never happy, are they?

I must admit, it's somewhat later than I'd anticipated as the salesman, Arthur, insisted on explaining every little thing to me. Honest, I could have just read the handbook when I got home. I didn't really follow too much of it but I did pick up that it takes quite some time to recharge the battery. I think he said 4 to 5 minutes. About the same time it takes to drink a milkshake – preferably chocolate.

There's a small dial here that shows me how the battery is doing. Hmm – it does seem to be going down quite a bit. In fact, rather a lot. Arthur said he had never heard of Godalming but I've read that some electric cars can do about 200 miles per charge and Godalming is only about 180 miles away. Make that 160 as I speak. Maybe I should speed up a bit as there seem to be quite a few cars behind me and it is starting to get dark. And it's raining. Still, I'm heading south so it should all be downhill from now on.

In fact, the battery is running down quite fast now. I'm no mathematician but I have a feeling that I might not quite make it unless I slow down (as Arthur explained it does more miles the slower you go) or find somewhere I can recharge. Looking at the growing queue behind me on this single carriageway and the not infrequent hooting, I probably shouldn't slow down too much. I don't want to annoy too many other drivers on my first solo trip.

By now it's clear that, unfortunately, I will have to find somewhere to recharge. I spot a layby ahead and pull in much to the relief of my fellow-travellers: one of whom seems to shout something at me as he passes. I don't think it was complimentary. My challenge now is to work out which of the many dials on the keyboard actually tells me where the recharging points are. A good time, perhaps, to look at the handbook. It takes me a while but eventually I find the answer and press the button. It looks as though there is one but it's not that close. However, I should be able to make it before the battery gives up. Now that would be unfortunate. I realise that I've never actually used a satnav before but it seems clear enough where to go. It's not actually on this road so I need to take the next but one turning on the left.

So far so good although it does seem a rather quiet road. It seems to go on and on as it snakes its way through the darkening countryside. I'm beginning to feel somewhat concerned. What if, somehow, it's not down this road? By now it really is quite dark. And I realise I'm feeling quite hungry. I only had a yoghurt for lunch as I anticipated being home in Godalming for tea and a delicious shepherd's pie. My favourite.

What's that just ahead? Ah, yes, this looks like the place. I can see a couple of petrol pumps but no sign of a recharging point. In truth I'm not totally sure what one of them looks like. I stop and get out but the place looks deserted. 'Hello! Is anyone there?' I shout. No reply. I look at the pumps: they both appear to be locked. Then I spot a small shop with its light on but, when I try the door, I find it's locked. I try shouting again just in case but it's evident there's no one around. Still, the gizmo showed there is a recharging point here somewhere so I've just got to find it. I walk around the fairly small area twice but cannot see anything remotely resembling my quarry. Now it really is quite dark. And cold. At least it's not rain… What was that? Yes, now it is raining. I go and sit in the car.

There's little charge left in the battery so I turn everything off and sit in the dark and think. This is not what I'd anticipated when I went electric. I look for my mobile phone though I'm not sure whom to phone for assistance. Here it is. I turn it on but – as I feared – it's quite dead.

It's 9.13pm and I'm not sure what to do. Presumably the garage will open tomorrow morning but I really don't fancy sitting here all night. All is quiet – apart from my stomach rumbling.

Hey, what's this? Car headlights! Perhaps I should get out and flag them down as it's unlikely they're going to stop here at a closed garage. But – hold on – they seem to be turning in! They are. Maybe they've seen me?

'Are you OK mate?'

'Not exactly,' I reply.

'What's the problem? Broken down?'

'In a way. This is an electric car and I need to recharge the battery. I believe there's a recharging point here but I just can't find it.'

'There certainly is, mate. That's why I've stopped. Mine's electric too. Here, I'll show you where it is.'

He drives slowly behind the shop and there it is. Just the one.

'It's very well hidden isn't it? I'd never have found it. Thank-goodness you stopped.'

I go to get my car. On my return, I see he is already charging his car.

'Sorry I went first, mate, but I'm in a bit of a hurry. It's my cat's birthday.'

'No problem,' I reply. 'What's another 5 minutes between fellow electric car owners, eh?'

'5 minutes? More like 45 minutes, mate. That's the one disadvantage. It takes a long time to recharge.'

45 minutes! Before I can even start to recharge. By now it's raining quite heavily so I go to sit in my car.

'I'll beep when I'm done,' he says with a smile.

I'm just nodding off when I hear the beep. I look up and see him wave as he drives off. I check my watch: 10:19. At this rate, I won't be back in Godalming before midnight. I try to start the car but nothing happens. The battery is completely drained. I'll have to push it round to the recharging point.

That was easier said than done. It took me a while to realise it's easier to push a car when the brake's not on. And steering it around a corner in between pushes is harder than it sounds. Still, I've made it. Here we are beside the recharging point. But what's this? There appear to be two connectors to plug into and they look quite different from each other. Which one did he use? I didn't notice. Perhaps only one will fit? I try the first one and – halleluiah! – it fits! Maybe my luck has turned at last. Yes, it seems to be recharging. What a relief! Just 45 minutes to go…

But then it stops. After just 5 minutes. Surely it's not finished? Have I got an ultra-fast battery? I don't recall Arthur telling me that. I look for something to press but can't see anything. Mind you, in this darkness, I can't see much at all. I check the battery and it's still almost empty. So why has it suddenly stopped? And what do I do? Perhaps, I conclude, I'm using the wrong slot after all. I'll try the other one.

The problem is that I can't get the hose thing out. I try juggling it and even shouting at it but nothing works. The car is stuck fast! By now I'm starting to get desperate. Why is early adopting so difficult? This is so unfair! Here I am trying to save the planet and this happens.

Was that thunder? I think it was. By now it's absolutely bucketing down. I get into the car. It's so cold. And I'm so hungry. This could be a very long night unless, somehow, I manage to get to sleep. But that seems very unlikely…

'You OK, guv?'

Someone is rapping on the window. I look up at a friendly face. It's light. Clearly, I did manage to doze.

'Nice car! Have you just bought it then?'

'Yesterday. I was driving it home when the battery ran out.'

'Where's home then?'

'Godalming. In Surrey.'

'Really? I had a cousin lived in Godalming. Till his accident. Quite a long way to go still. Now, I must admit, I don't know too much about electric cars – as you can see, my Mercedes is petrol. So, let's see what the problem is.'

He went over to the recharging point and examined it for a moment or so and then did something which – miraculously – freed the hose. Then he put it into the other hole and the whole thing started up again. Quite what he'd done, I had no idea.

'That's fantastic! Thank you so much!' I gushed. I should have asked him to show me just what he'd done but you can't think of everything.

He disappeared into the shop and wished me 'Good luck!'

So here I am, 45 minutes later. I'm driving along at 43 mph. This time, I'm heading for the Midlands rather than Godalming. Hopefully I can find that car showroom again. I'm going to ask Arthur if he will buy it back. No more early-adopting for me. I've learned my lesson. This time I'll let the train take the strain. And have a huge breakfast!

Godalming Events

Post War 1970– 1984
1984 - Godalming twinned with Joigny, France.
1982 – Beaver Scouts started.
1980 – Godalming Photographic Club formed.
1977 – Godalming twinned with Mayen, Germany.
1970 – Godalming Wool Fayre.

TWO CATS IN WITLEY - THE END OF TINKER'S TALE

by Christine Butler

My constant companion has gone. Fallen asleep for the final time. She had what my extra special person Christine called a fit and the vet man came to see her. 'I'm sorry,' he said, shaking his head. 'There's nothing I can do. Unless I operate on her damaged spine she won't walk again. And she's too old to cope with the operation.' I miss that annoying cat, although she complained a lot. We shared all the problems of life in the Aldershot house and we both thought that it was a pity we couldn't have come to our lovely home in Witley straight from Horsham.

Christine said that Wendy used to make a fuss because of the problem she had with her spine and the pain it caused. I suppose that was why she wasn't as good at running and climbing as me. I used to tease her by dashing up a tree, watching as she followed me, and then scrambling down leaving her stuck there. She usually clambered down backwards, very carefully and miaowing loudly.

She didn't have the pain when she started following me out into the garden through the small window in the lean-to. She was still a kitten and Christine didn't think she'd manage to get out when she left her shut in the kitchen of our Horsham home while she and Len were away for the day. The young rascal would jump down onto the dustbin below the window and return the same way, making sure that she was safely back inside when they came home from work. One day Christine arrived home early and was upset not to find Wendy indoors. Having greeted her I meowed to go out and led her to where Wendy was sunning herself in the garden. 'How did you get there, you naughty cat?' Christine exclaimed.

Soon after that Christine heard Wendy calling loudly in the garden for a mate. 'That cat's too young to have kittens,' she commented to Len, my other very special person. 'She'll have to be done.' It meant a visit to the vet man for her. She came home smelling of the vet's and with a patch of her soft grey fur missing. I avoided her till the smell wore off.

Sometime later I was grateful for her watchfulness in the garden. I was out hunting two gardens away when the local bully-cat suddenly sprang up onto the wall where I was sitting and confronted me. His language was appalling. I growled back but was too scared to move. Wendy heard the noise from our garden and ran indoors for help. She wailed for Christine, then kept going into the garden and back to the kitchen until Christine followed to see what she was fussing about. Christine heard the swearing and spotted me crouching on the wall where I was cornered. 'Oh Tinker,' she said loudly, picked up something and threw it at the cat, taking him by surprise. It hit the wall just below him. He shot off giving me the chance to dash to the safety of my own garden.

I missed the small, walled gardens at Horsham when we moved away. The gardens where we lived in Aldershot were extensive but very exposed, with fences instead of walls and few trees or large bushes. The local cats could spot me easily, being bright ginger, and there was little cover for hunting. The area and the neighbours were noisier than in Horsham, with children next door. Wendy liked them but I didn't.

I took an instant dislike to our new home because of finding another cat living there when we moved in. The little tabby had been living wild and spotted the chance of a home of his own when he heard the sounds of stuff being moved in. The front door was open so he ran in and tried to make friends with Len and Christine by getting under their feet. He refused to go so in the end they decided to adopt him, giving him the name Captain Hook. When Wendy and I arrived a few days later he had a surprise, not being the only cat living there after all, but he still wouldn't go. At least he was a friendly cat. He learnt to play with us gradually, not previously knowing how.

Like Wendy, he used to go next door to see the children. He said he thought they loved him and wanted him to live with them but he was settled with us by then. When the family moved away he wasn't asked to go with them. However, one evening when Christine and Len were out late in the car they came back. I was indoors but Wendy and Captain watched under our side gate as they emptied a tin of food onto the front step. Pleased to see them and the food,

Captain squeezed under the gate and ran to greet them. While he was eating they scooped him up and put him in a box to take to their car. We never saw him again.

Christine and Len were cross when they came home to find an opened tin of cat food on the front step and no Captain. The food had been roughly put back into the tin with some leaves as well so they guessed what had happened without needing to understand Wendy's complaints. Len commented that he would have let the little stray cat go with them if they had asked.

At last we made another and final move. After a few days staying with two of my special people, where we visited sometimes, we arrived in Witley. At first I thought we were on holiday and would have to go back to the house in Aldershot when it was over. I heard Christine express that feeling too.

Exploring the house and peering out through the windows, we quickly found there was a large garden surrounding it, with lots of bushes and trees. 'What small creatures live out there to be chased and caught?' I wondered. But Christine and Len wouldn't let us out to see. Wendy and I both made our thoughts known about that. We ran from window to window meowing loudly. I pawed at the glass, insisting I was going out. They eventually gave in and opened a door, following us as we dashed out with prrreows of joy.

It took us a long time to inspect the garden, smelling where other cats had been and picking up the scent of creatures we didn't recognise. We heard rustlings in fallen leaves and lots of birds. Eventually hunger sent us back indoors and I tried to let Christine and Len know how much I liked the garden. I think they understood. 'You can go out again tomorrow, Tinker,' Christine said, stroking me. 'It'll be dark soon. Better not chance meeting other cats in the gloom.' I didn't convince her that I'd be safe enough. I can see quite well in the dark. Feeling sleepy after all the excitement, I curled up on a comfy chair for a nap.

Next day we woke up early, ready to continue our adventures in the exciting garden. This was the start of a very happy time for the two of us, spoiled for just a short time by the attentions of another bully-cat. He soon found a home and his own special person several gardens away and didn't come into ours very often after that.

People visited us sometimes. I liked most of them and would ask to be stroked and played with by saying 'prrreow' and rubbing against their legs. Wendy was not so sociable and often kept her distance. If I didn't like the visitors I'd hide in a bedroom or go out.

Len and Christine gradually tidied the garden, then dug holes and moved things. A large store with a wide, solid pathway to it was built, to put the cars and other things in. I worked out how to reach its roof by climbing the oak tree near it and jumping across. One day when my people were out, I chanced the leap across from that roof to the house roof.

Something called moss grows on part of that roof and my claws gripped it easily. The top of the smaller, lower section made a great lookout and I was still there when Len and Christine returned. Being met by just Wendy, Christine asked her, 'Where's Tinker? Is she alright?'

The cat replied by looking up at the house. When Christine followed her gaze she suddenly spotted me and exclaimed, 'How on earth did she get up there! Oh, Len look where she is. The ridge isn't level. I've never noticed that before.' It led to strange men banging about in the loft later and a chance for me to find mice up there amongst the cobwebs and boxes. I had to jump up from the top of a stepladder put up in the hall.

Wendy sometimes did daft things. We both had favourite places in the garden where we could sit and watch what was going on. Mine was a branch in the centre of a low bush with big, shiny leaves not far from the back of the house. Christine referred to it as 'Tinker's laurel'. Late one evening I was hiding there when I heard a noise like a dog in a hurry. I froze and watched as something brown and furry with a big bushy tail rushed past, down the garden path and over the fence at the bottom. To my astonishment, close behind it ran a small grey furry cat!

She couldn't keep up, thank goodness, stopped when I hissed a warning at her and then sat down for an embarrassed wash. Christine and Len were in the kitchen at the time and also heard the paws running. They said later that they thought it was a fox and that

Wendy was lucky it hadn't stopped and turned on her.

Why didn't we move straight here from Horsham, instead of going to Aldershot first, I wonder sometimes. Len and Christine had their reasons, of course. We've been very happy in this Witley house with no upstairs and its wonderful gardens to hunt and play in. But recently I've started to visit the vet-man more often. When I feel ill and weak and don't want to eat he jabs me with his needle and I feel almost kittenish again for a while.

Now those visits have increased and my weakness is worse. Len and Christine talk about problems with my kidneys. Perhaps my time is nearly up and, like Wendy, I will soon go to sleep for the final time.

FOOTNOTE

I first started writing down Tinkerbell's thoughts in 1969 but stopped again in 1972 when we were planning to move away from Horsham. My manuscript languished in a cupboard, neglected for years except for some notes added about young Captain. Eventually in 2005 I joined a local Creative Writing class with the intention of finishing the story. It needed completely re-writing, which I finished in 2011 but without adding the Aldershot years when Tinker was so often unhappy. Now her story is concluded. She was 17 when she died in 1985 and Wendy was 15.

Godalming Events

War and Inter-war 1914-1945

1945 – Farncombe Wanderers Cricket Club formed.

1937 – Railway electrified.

1937 – Godalming Band formed to play for coronation of King George VI.

1936 – Rotary Club of Godalming formed (now two clubs).

1935 – The Regal Cinema opened in Meadrow.

1934 – Guildford and Godalming by-pass opened.

THE WARNING

by Julie Buckingham

It was a warm night in the Surrey countryside of 1759, and the dark kerchief he wore to disguise his lower features felt hot and muggy tied around the back of his neck.

He sweated in his well-dressed finery, his bunch of lace at his chin, choking him in the warm, balmy night air, his coat of claret velvet and brown breeches lay heavy on his skin. His right hand felt weighed down through holding his flintlock pistol so tightly, as he strained to hear the clip-clop, clip-clop of horse's hooves, amidst the slight rustle of the leaves in the copse he was hiding in.

And then, a movement caught his ruby brown eyes and he spurred his mount, Robin, from the hidden hollow and out into the path of a small horse-drawn buggy, his pistol held high in his sweaty palm.

'Stand and deliver your purse! I'll take your money or your life!' The strident order rang out on that fatal still summer's evening.

The old, rough-looking buggy the girls were travelling in came to a creaking halt.

The smaller girl – little more than a child, had been half asleep, jolted, and yet somehow soothed by the buggy's lurching, swaying journey to Godalming.

The highwayman pointed his pistol in the other girl's direction. She looked older and had been driving the buggy.

'Please climb down from the coach so that I can see whom I have way-laid!'

At that moment the moon came out, and the highwayman saw two scared young faces staring fixedly at him with open mouths.

The older girl stepped down from the buggy's wooden seat. 'Stay there!' she warned the younger girl.

Blinking hard, she wrung her hands together and spoke tremulously. 'Please, sir – spare us! We are unarmed and in a terrible rush to reach Godalming!'

Wide awake now, the smaller girl fastened frightened blue eyes upon the highwayman, gasping at his rapier and menacing flintlock pistol.

The highwayman pointed his weapon at her pale face. She had freckles and silvery-gold hair, and she reminded him of someone.

He cried: 'Aha! Who have we here? Your name, I pray, before I take your goods!'

The little thing replied stoutly, despite her pumping heart. 'I – I am Beth Wilcox, and we are carrying no goods, sir!'

Had she imagined it, but at the spouting of her name, the highwayman seemed suddenly surprised, and for the space of a heartbeat, he hesitated and pointed his pistol away from her young, worried face.

'Beth Wilcox?' He sounded her name on his tongue wonderingly, then he frowned. 'Why, in God's name are you both out so late at night?'

The older girl said: 'We were travelling for help to get a doctor for my mistress – she has been taken ill.'

'What is wrong with your mistress? What is wrong with her?' The questions came sharply from his mouth.

'We do not know; she has pain, and a high fever!'

The highwayman's broad, agile shoulders seemed to slump. He frowned again, then hesitated, and the girl driver took advantage of his uncertainty to say swiftly: 'Sir, please let us go on our mission of mercy. My mistress may be dying for all I know!'

She was surprised to see a flash of fear in those ruby brown eyes, and a deep sigh exploded from his mouth. 'Then go! Travel swiftly to Godalming. There is a doctor Hicks in the main street... I'll not stand in your way. Go swiftly!'

'Thank you, sir.' The older girl ascended the buggy to take the reins again.

The highwayman walked over to Beth's side of the buggy. She shrank away from him.

'Little Beth, I mean you no harm. Do not be afraid of me! Please, continue your journey! I hope we may meet again – under better circumstances hopefully, than tonight!'

White-faced, she nodded once, and then the buggy lurched forwards, leaving the young girl wondering what the highwayman's words had meant...

*****

The old tumble-down cottage where the sick Marie Wilcox lived was the first dwelling down a narrow, rutted lane that led on to a small hamlet.

The doctor had at last been to visit her, thanks to her daughter and young maiden storming off to get him. Dr Hicks had found her to be in serious, heavy pain in her left side. He had bled her, using leeches, then had applied a mixture of castor, Valerian, camphor and Opium Dissolved, to the affected area. For a draught for her to take he mixed up an ungodly concoction of ten grams of Nitre with Hartshorn Salts, a sufficient quality of lemon juice, forty drops each of Thebaic Tincture, Crocus Castor, Virginia Snakeroot and Antimonial Wine in a sufficient quantity of Simple Syrup.

Normally, to the genteel folk, Dr Hicks would have charged a whopping two guineas, but to this widow who lived only with her ten-year-old daughter and young maiden, he charged a couple of shillings for his night's work. He promised he would be in to see her again the next evening and left.

On his way from the hamlet he was accosted by a gentleman on a dark horse, who rode out from nowhere onto the rutted lane the doctor was travelling home on.

'A fine night, Dr Hicks! How is your evening so far?'

The stranger had taken his Tricorn hat off and, in the moonlight, Dr Hicks recognised him.

'Why, it's Jack Mansfield from the Manor House! My goodness, you startled me! I didn't recognise you wearing that hat! Yes – yes; my day has not ended yet, I'm afraid! I didn't know you were back from the war.'

'Temporary leave. I was at the battle of Jumonville in May and ended up an injured beggar! Had a three month stay in hospital.'

'I am sorry to hear that. You look quite well now!'

'I am much rested, thank-you. I hear Edward Boscawen has greatly weakened the French Mediterranean fleet at Lagos? It should ensure the British fleet's supremacy over the French!'

'Yes, magnificent news! Er, the war reminds me, how is your father keeping now? He has his own battle with his health, doesn't he?'

'Very unhealthy, I'm afraid. He will keep drinking his port even though he knows it's bad for his gout!'

'I'll drop by at the end of the week. Remember me to him!'

Jack Mansfield nodded, then said: 'I hear one of my workers, Marie Wilcox is ill?'

'That is correct, but I have managed to get her fever down!'

'What's the problem?'

'Abdominal pain on her left-hand side. I expect you're wondering when she'll be fit for work at the Manor again, what?'

'I am. How is she really?'

'You seem very concerned for the young woman?'

'I am her employer. I want her back at work as soon as possible!'

'Of course you do! She's weak at the moment, but she's young. She'll pull through!'

'Thank-you, Doctor, would you like me to escort you to Godalming? These highways and hills are lonely places at night!'

'I'll manage... Although they do say there is a highwayman at large around here...?'

'Really?' Jack's ruby brown eyes widened. 'You don't say?'

'Just a rumour, I expect. Mind you don't bump into him on your way to the Manor House! Ha!'

'I'll be careful, Doctor.'

'Right! I'll be off, then.'

They parted, but Jack remained seated on his horse. When he was satisfied that the doctor had really ridden off in the darkness, he made his way to Marie Wilcox's cottage...

Marie lay abed. Her ten-year-old daughter and young maiden, Margaret, were sleeping next door. There came a soft scratching at her casement window. It didn't worry her. She strove quickly to unlatch the window, joy in her heart, delighted he had arrived to see her.

'My love! I feared you would never come!' She wound her arms around the highwayman in familiar surrender. He breathed into her red silvery hair, and laughed up at her blue, blue eyes, and they kissed lingeringly.

'How are you now? Any better?'

'Better for seeing you after such a long, long time!'

'My injuries from the war stopped me from coming to you sooner! Are you in any pain?'

'Only slightly. I've been told to rest and eat grains and veg but no meat.'

'I'll come again, tomorrow night.'

'Not tomorrow – the doctor is visiting me again!'

'I'll arrive after the doctor's been. Can I do anything to help you?'

'Yes, you can! To please me, will you stop being a highwayman? The King's men roam the heath now, looking, searching... I am so afraid you'd be caught and hung at Tyburn! I cannot bear to think of your beautiful body being strung up on a gibbet for everyone to jeer at! I love you too much!'

'Don't worry about me. Just keep our child safe! She is growing into a very pretty young woman. I didn't recognise her this evening. Not until she told me her full name! It was a shock to confront my daughter in the dark, I can tell you! I was that worried for her – if anything had happened to you, what would I have done?'

'You would have had to adopt her!'

'Marie – you are my life! But you know I have no room for a ten-year old in my world, dashing around the countryside at night, scaring and worrying folk like I do!'

'I agree with you there! You seem to have this mad desire to be a highwayman! You have not seen me for over two years, having been away and injured, and our child, you have not seen her for the last five years!'

'I know... and I've thought long and hard about her. I may be called away again soon, to fight the French. I've been considering giving her my name and making an honest woman out of you!'

'Oh Jack, such talk thrills me! But if you were to get killed, and I were to become ill again – what, then? We must think of someone we could leave her with...'

'Your young friend, Margaret, and her family would have her. At least if I paid them! They know and like Beth. I'll write a letter to them tonight and send it tomorrow via one of my grooms!'

'But what of your father? He would never agree that we…'

'Shhh!' He reached upward and placed his hand across her mouth. 'I hear something! Someone is abroad tonight! I must go! We will talk more of this tomorrow night!'

'Oh, Jack – be careful!'

He grinned. 'As ever! 'Till tomorrow night, sweetheart. Be here!' And he was gone.

*****

Unknown to the two lovers, the doctor had returned to the cottage for a medical item which he had left behind.

He'd seen and heard the couple talking and making their plans.

He wasn't a vindictive doctor, and he liked Jack Mansfield, but he was truthful, and he went and told an acquaintance of his, a magistrate, who in turn forewarned the army...

*****

The following evening Marie was out of bed. She still had the pain after the doctor's short visit, (he seemed in a hurry to leave), but it wasn't so bad now, and she was even able to hum a little tune whilst waiting for her lover's return. But what was that noise? An urgent thudding on her cottage door, as if a thousand soldiers were camped outside?

Bidding young Beth and Margaret to stay back, Marie cautiously opened the top part of her cottage stable door.

A tall soldier with a musket surveyed her contemptuously. 'Stand aside, woman, we are coming in!'

He pushed past her, ignoring her shock and dismay. She looked to the other two girls with alarm in her eyes, which they reflected back. Other troops entered after him, until, it seemed, the tiny living room was full of armed soldiers.

'Perhaps you was expectin' someone else?' the lead soldier sneered.

'No, not at all. I'm alone with my family!'

'You lie, madam! I put it to you, you are expectin' a highwayman to arrive here later, eh?'

'A highwayman?!' The young maid Margaret echoed wonderingly. 'But, sir, one such held us up last night!'

'Did he, miss? So how is it you've lived to tell the tale?'

'Margaret glanced at Marie's set face. She said lamely: 'I don't know. He just let us go!'

Marie's throat was dry and prickly. 'No, no! Please believe me – we are not expecting…'

'But, yes, you are: and we'll wait with you, and catch him! Bind her – and the other females, so they can't escape to raise the alarm!'

Hot hands applied rope around her trembling wrists. 'Please – my daughter, surely you don't have to tie her up too?'

The lead soldier smirked. 'I'm taking no chances with you or anyone here. 'You look a cunning little minx to me. I'd not be doing my job if I didn't tie everyone up!'

The two women and the one child were hustled into a corner of the room, with their backs to the rickety cottage staircase. Right behind Marie, she knew, was an old British Land Pattern Musket that she used for shooting rabbits. It was hidden in the shadows under the well of the stairs, and she had primed it ready this very morning.

If only she could reach it, she might alert her lover.

The house clock chimed midnight.

And then, along the rutted lane leading to the hamlet, her keen ears picked up the sound she dreaded to hear... Jack and his trusty steed, riding hell for leather to reach her, coming closer, closer. Oh, it was too late! Too late! She could think of only one thing she could do.

Any minute now the soldiers at her windows would open fire at him.

She prayed to her God and gently turned around and, with tied hands in front of her, found her weapon.

All eyes were on the lane leading to her cottage.

She picked up the fire-arm with two trembling hands. It was very heavy to pick up with tied hands, but she was strong and despair helped her. She did not notice how hard her daughter watched her with her little bright blue eyes full of wonder and fear, for tears were falling from her mother's face.

Marie somehow managed to position the long weapon under her chin and gulped, once, her fingers straining for the trigger...

*****

Jack was riding swiftly towards his true love, thinking of her and what he was going to do for her. That very morning, he had already sent a note to Margaret's people via his head groom, begging them to watch over Beth should anything happen to Marie, and he had enclosed some coins. He was blissfully unaware of the drama being played out in Marie's cottage.

In the stillness of a hot summer's night a single shot rang out, followed by panicky screams.

Alerted and shocked, he swung his horse away from the path instinctively. Blinkered by the sudden command, Robin spun into a thicket hedge, dislodging his rider. Jack lost his stirrups and flew over his horse's head, at the same time as a volley of musket shots zeroed in on his moonlit figure.

A musket ball lodged in Jack's heart, and he died straight away, just as Marie had done, trying to warn him of the danger with her death.

Godalming Events

War and Inter-war 1914-1945
1930 – Godalming County School opened.
1925 – Godalming Operatic Society formed.
1921 – Public Museum proposed in upper portion of old town hall – Pepperpot.
1914 – Phillips Memorial opened.

THE BUTTERFLY EFFECT
by Paul Rennie

Dermott Connor was what is known as a 'bad'un'. He was one of those tradespeople who, if they can get away with it, lie and cheat their way through life, leaving a trail of disgruntled customers in their wake. He ran what was laughingly called a handyman business, and thought nothing of overcharging and cutting corners on the shoddy work that provided his main source of income. The motto on his business flyers was *'No job too small'*, although it omitted the *'No bill too large'* part. Over-running costs, a fake receipt here, an over-inflated quote there, were his *modus operandi*, and all cash in hand, although he was very careful to charge VAT, which of course he pocketed along with his mostly tax-free income.

He had acquired an old cottage just off Meadrow between Godalming and Guildford. It was a former alms house, and Mrs Marshall, the elderly lady he had bought it off, had lived there many years without feeling the need to modernize the dwelling. Dermott had bought the house from her when she was moved by social services into a nursing home. He was in pole position to buy the house because he knew her through the numerous odd jobs he had done, and overcharged her for, over the years. He had been waiting for this opportunity, and had succeeded in getting the place for a low price, mainly because the structural survey revealed a lot of defects, most of which were a direct result of his past shoddy work. As a consequence of the sale price she received, Mrs Marshall's savings ran out rather quickly when she had to pay the monthly fees at the privately run *Twilight Path* nursing home, and she was moved to a cheaper local authority home, where she survived only 2 weeks. This didn't bother Dermott. He immediately started renovating the cottage, with the objective of making a quick profit. He had no intention of living there because, after all, he had a perfectly good council property across town.

After a year he had almost completed the work and, because it was his own place and he wanted a premium price, he had spent considerably more care and attention on the refurbishment than his normal work, and even used some of the quality fittings that he had billed, but not necessarily fitted, in his customers' jobs. Dermott was just finishing off the kitchen with its new oak cupboards and shiny new appliances. He was trying to get the under-sink unit to fit, a job complicated by the cut-outs that were required to allow the water and waste pipes to pass through the back of the unit. This is where his old work practices re-emerged. He measured and marked on the laminate where he thought the pipes would line up, and cut the openings with a hole cutter. They didn't quite fit. The hot and cold-water pipe holes were about right, but the bigger waste pipe hole just didn't line up when he offered up the unit. Swearing, he pulled the cupboard back out and widened the hole with a jig saw. He pushed the cupboard back, but it still didn't line up. He swore again more profanely, and cut a bit more out of the back of the unit in an elongated arc. He tried to force the unit back in. It was still slightly tight. He pulled the unit back out, but because it almost fitted, the pipes caught the edges of the holes, and jammed. He pulled with all his might, and it suddenly released with an almighty crack. He looked at the back of the unit, and a large circular piece of laminated chipboard had broken away, leaving a gaping hole at the back of the cabinet. The piece of white chipboard looked like a sneering face with two eyes where the water pipe holes were drilled, and a smirking grinning mouth formed by the waste pipe hole. It looked like it was laughing at him. He kicked it across the floor and ranted at the world, then retrieved it and offered it up to the hole in the cabinet. He considered gluing it back, but the edges were too jagged, and too many small fragments had fallen off. In the end he did what came naturally to him, and bodged it by cutting a big circular hole to make it look like it was deliberate. After all, who looks at the back of kitchen cupboards when buying a house? He threw the offending piece of chipboard onto the pile of old tiles and assorted rubble that had accumulated from the work. Having finished the kitchen, he filled six sacks with the debris, and put them in the back of his van.

Later that afternoon, he drove to Witley tip, or Witley Community Recycling Centre, as it is now known. Now the tip had undergone a bit of a refurbishment itself, and whereas, in the past, he had been able to sling anything that he could fit in his van into the skips, including, it must be said, the odd sheet of asbestos, he was confronted by a large man in a fluorescent jacket who insisted on inspecting the load. In spite of Dermott's protestations that it was just household waste, the man insisted that there would be a charge of £4 for each sack of material and a further £12 for some plaster board. Dermott refused point blank and, after arguing, fist waving and threatening to write to the Council, drove out of the site with the bags still in the back. He contemplated dumping them in the lane on the way out, but thought that there might be CCTV cameras, and that the fly-tipping might be traced back to him.

He bided his time and later, at 2 o'clock in the morning, he drove out again looking for somewhere he could jettison the load for free. Somewhere it wouldn't be seen for some time. Somewhere like the River Wey. The section of river through Godalming was much too busy and brightly lit, even at those hours, so he needed a quieter more discreet place upstream. He drove towards Milford and turned off down the lane to the small hamlet of Eashing. There he saw the perfect spot on the ancient bridge over the river. There were a few houses nearby, but all of the lights were off and honest folk were asleep. He parked in a little pull-in just before the bridge, switched off his headlights, and waited in the dark. All was quiet and there was no sign of any cars approaching. He drove up onto the bridge, and with the engine running, jumped out, and quickly emptied the sacks one by one into the dark swirling water below, finishing by hurling the pieces of plaster board over the parapet. It disappeared quickly, leaving no sign of his handiwork. He drove back to Godalming, and went to bed, pleased with a good night's work. Surprisingly, for that much debris, there was little to show for his action. The plasterboard disintegrated, and the cement and grout dispersed, just leaving the water a little murky. The tiles and chipboard sank to the bottom where they slowly tumbled along downstream in the current.

Now I forgot to mention that behind the old alms houses there is a stream, appropriately called Hell Ditch. It actually forms a small bypass loop of the River Wey, leaving it near Westbrook Mills, and re-joining it opposite Broadwater Park. It is part of the complex flood defence system that allows excess water to drain onto the Lammas lands to act as a buffer to prevent flooding of the town. Normally, Hell Ditch is just a tiny stream hidden by undergrowth so that you'd hardly notice it. In times of heavy rain this changes and it becomes one of the routes for excess water from the river to bypass the built-up parts of the town. In 1968 there was serious flooding in the area and Guildford was particularly badly hit; especially at the bottom of the High Street near the river. In 2013/2014, after another wet winter, it was Godalming's turn for major flooding, this time partly due to a decision to protect Guildford by attempting to hold the floodwater upstream. After the clear up and outcry, the Council decided it was time to spend the money on updating the defences with new flood walls and sluices at Meadrow and Catteshall, and these were duly installed.

Now back to the present. You recall that Dermott had tipped his building waste into the River Wey at Eashing. What he hadn't considered is the consequence of his actions and where that rubbish could end up. As in chaos theory, and the proverbial butterfly beating its wings in the Amazon jungle and influencing the weather, there were indeed weather-related consequences to Dermott's thoughtless action. Over the course of a few days the debris made its way downstream towards Godalming, pausing occasionally in little pools and by-waters, but always heading relentlessly towards the sea. Amongst the material drifting along the bottom was the piece of laminated chipboard from the back of the kitchen unit. Being essentially wood, it drifted slightly faster than the heavier material, and formed the vanguard of the flotilla advancing on the town. At some time over the ensuing days, it reached one of the new sluice gates, knocked against the metal plates, twisted, and wedged itself in the opening. The remaining debris finally caught up and formed ranks behind the chipboard creating a strong and effective dam. Usually this wouldn't matter too much because it would have eventually been spotted and cleared and the normal flow rate through the Hell Ditch sluice was very low.

However, out in the Atlantic, a severe storm had been brewing and had got big enough to be given a name; Storm Beyonce, presumably because they were running out of more traditional names. Three weeks earlier, about the time Dermott was fly tipping, a butterfly in the Brazilian rainforest was quietly supping its breakfast nectar from an orchid. This would have been irrelevant to our story except that it was a Blue Morpho, one of the largest butterflies in the world. It had drained the nectar from deep within the flower and withdrew its proboscis, coiling it up neatly under its chin, ready for moving on to the next orchid. As it launched itself into the air it spotted a tree frog lurking with intent. The butterfly performed an evasive banking turn, and in doing so created little vortices of air from its wing beats. The tiny draught of wind extended upwards and outwards causing a minute change in air pressure.

Above the tree canopy, a layer of cooler drier air had trapped the warm moisture emanating from the trees, like the thin membrane of a bubble. The tiny gust of wind from the butterfly was just enough to disrupt the barrier and make a tiny hole in it. Like a pin-pricked balloon, the warm moist air which, until then had been held back, escaped through the hole making it larger until a plume of moisture-laden air poured into the upper atmosphere. The pocket of air cooled, the water in it condensed, and this formed a small cloud which joined with others to create a cumulonimbus. As the new cloud drifted eastwards, it grew and started to rotate, gathering energy and moisture, and moving up the Beaufort scale. Reaching the Atlantic and heading north eastwards, and after a brief circuit of the Caribbean, it joined with similar clouds to reach storm force. Thus, Beyonce was born. She followed the route of the Gulf stream towards the British Isles carrying with her a lot of water which, over the next few days, she

110

poured as torrential rain over the South of England, particularly in the Surrey Hills area.

With that much rain, the rivers steadily rose, and the flood defences were duly activated. All but one. The sluice gate at Hell Ditch failed to close, jammed open by the debris that had collected in it. It wasn't noticed because the temporary dam formed by Dermott's selfish act held back the water flow. By the time it was noticed it was too late. The dam had given way and the pent-up floodwater behind it poured through unopposed into Hell Ditch, which was transformed from a small stream into a raging torrent. The muddy flood waters surged downstream like the Severn Bore and quickly overflowed the bank, crossed over the rear gardens and poured into the houses on Meadrow, including Dermott's newly renovated cottage.

Dermott tried desperately to stop the water coming in with sandbags and bailing with buckets but to no avail. The filthy water rose to three feet deep in the cottage carrying with it assorted silt and debris and totally destroying his whole year's work. Within a few days the problem with the defences was sorted out and the waters started to subside. The damage, however, was devastating and nothing on the ground floor could be saved. Dermott was left with a huge costly job to clear up the mess, dry out the property and start all over again.

Now most sensible people would have had insurance against this sort of act of God, but not Dermott. As I mentioned, he liked to take risks and cut corners. When he had inquired about insurance, the quotes were very high because of previous flooding events at the property. He had assumed that because of the new defences, flooding wouldn't occur again round there, and that the premiums would be lower. Insurance companies, however, tend to be a bit more pragmatic, and considered it still a high-risk area. Dermott decided that because of the high premium, he wouldn't bother with the insurance. Besides, he was selling the place soon anyway. Happily, the owners of the adjacent properties were wiser and more cautious, and were able to claim the full cost of repairs and reinstatement. As a result, Dermott was the only resident who had to bear the full cost of the repairs, which ran into tens of thousands of pounds.

The story doesn't quite end there. As Dermott cleared out the water, mud and river debris from his devastated kitchen, he spotted something white just underneath the water. He reached down and fished it out and wiped off the sludge with his sleeve. His face paled and he looked aghast as he recognized what he held in his hands. There staring up at him with its smirking grin was the piece of white laminated chipboard that he thought he had seen the back of.

THE FACE IN THE MIRROR
by Pauline North

Emma took a last look in the mirror. 'You'll do,' she told her reflection. The calm grey eyes in the mirror that had been critically assessing, crinkled at the corners, the face smiled. 'You are going to be one of those old ladies who talks to herself all day long.' She told her reflection.

She had taken particular note of the weather forecast: dry and warmer than average for May the forecaster had said, so she had dressed in a t-shirt and jeans. Practical for an afternoon working at Godalming's Spring Fair. There would be the small marquee to erect then tables to set out and all the boxes of donated bric-a-brac to arrange. She collected her bag on the way to the door and left.

As Emma drove past the Burys field, she saw that the fair was already taking shape with the large marquee on the far side already up and stalls and tents being set up all over the field.

Having parked, she made her way through the chaos avoiding the ice cream van because the driver was stopping for no-one in his rush to his pitch. Emma saw Jane and Tessa already in position so she hurried over to join them.

Jane met her with a smile. 'Thank goodness you're here; give us a hand with this frame Emm.'

The three of them wrestled with the telescopic legs on the frame of their marquee. 'We could do with another pair of hands.' Tessa muttered.

At last all four of the legs had clicked into place, the marquee was up. They stopped for a breather before tackling the tables.

'Didn't that new girl say she would try to get here Jane?'

'Who? What new girl?' Emma wanted to know.

'That's right, you missed the last meeting, a new recruit, a nice girl, about twenty. She moved into the area recently.' Then wistfully, 'we could do with some young people in the group, we're all knocking on a bit.'

'Stop it Jane, plenty of life left in us yet and anyway Emma is a generation younger than us.'

Emma grinned at the pair of them, old friends, they had been part of the fabric of Godalming for many years. When she had joined the small local charity four years ago they had made her welcome. For the first time in many years and after many moves to new towns or new villages she had felt settled.

An hour later the three of them stood back to admire their finished work, the fair would officially open soon and they were ready.

The warm weather had tempted the crowds out and the afternoon was off to a busy start. A little later

Emma turned from the customer she had just served to see a young woman standing at the end of the table, trying to attract attention. 'Hello, can I help you?'

'Well I planned to be here before the fair opened, I hope I'm not too late to be useful.'

'Ah, you must be the new volunteer, good. At the moment, until the first rush is over if you come round this side of the counter, you'll find that everything is priced so all you have to do is sell, oh and smile.'

When the first flush of customers had dispersed the newcomer said, 'Let me introduce myself, my name is Georgia.'

She smiled around the three women who introduced themselves in turn. 'I'm pleased to meet you all. I've brought some stuff along, perhaps one of you can help me, I have no idea what price to put on them.'

Tessa said, 'That sounds like a job for you Emma, you're very good at estimating value. While you're doing that Jane and I will go and get us all a drink, what would you like?'

With the choices noted the two women set off for the tea tent.

Most of the items in Georgia's bag were the usual mix of unwanted china, glass, a few books plus a rather nice photo frame.

'My mum donated all of those. I thought I'd bring this along; do you think this is something that will sell?'

She took out the last object from the bottom of the bag. Holding it as though it was fragile, she handed Emma a slender book. Emma took it from her and turned it over in her hands. It was obviously some years old though the cover showed only slight wear. Emma opened the cover and flicked through some of the pages.

'A volume of poetry, well it looks as though it's been well cared for.' She continued to study the open book. 'The inscription in the front, that was for you? This is your book?'

'Yes, that was written by my mum, my real mum. It was the only thing she left with me when she left me with the adoption agency. I have loved this book all my life; it has always been my connection to her. She must have chosen this gift to me so very carefully, if you read the poems all her love comes shining through.'

Emma looked at Georgia, studied the young face, it gave very little away only a slight tightening at the corners of her mouth, a sheen of tears in the grey eyes.

'Then why, why get rid of it?'

'For so long all I wanted was to find her so we could be reunited. Growing up I made up stories, imagined her living so many different lives, like perhaps she was struggling to bring up a large family,

116

feeling defeated by the hardship. I try to forget that one. Or maybe she found fame and fortune as an actress or she's a scientist. My favourite wish was that she has a loving husband, they live comfortably in a nice home and she is very happy. I imagined us talking endlessly, laughing at the same things. We would go shopping together.

'As I got older I started to realise that we can never mend that connection, we know nothing of each other's lives and that is how it has to stay. I will always have her and this book in my heart but now I am going to set her free.'

'What if you meet her some day?'

'I know it sounds cruel but I hope I don't.'

Emma closed the book. 'Well let me see, shall we say a pound as it's such a lovely book. Look don't put a sticky label on it, that would spoil the cover, I'll write the price very lightly in pencil, here on the inside of the cover. Sticky labels for the rest of the items though, if I give you a price you write it out and stick it on.'

The other two women arrived back with the drinks. 'Oh my god, we timed that badly didn't we Jane, I thought we would never reach the end of the queue, have you two been alright here?'

'We've been fine Tess, is that my tea? Thank you.'

A passer-by that fine afternoon, if they were to stroll up to the women's stall to take a look, would have been drawn into the happy atmosphere. A

117

steady stream of customers pondered their purchases, joined in the conversations and the laughter and left with a smile on their faces,

They were busy enough that no-one noticed Emma drop a few pounds into the cash box and slip the photo frame and the book of poems into her bag. A few minutes later she said, 'the afternoons almost over, how about a group photo to remember the day?'

She gathered them in front of the marquee and with her mobile carefully framed the shot, 'there, done.'

Tessa said, 'give me your phone, now you go and stand between Jane and Georgia.'

With that photo taken, almost reluctantly, the four of them started to pack all the left-over stock away. Jane went and brought her van onto the field and the marquee and all the boxes were packed inside, then she and Tessa climbed in and calling a last goodbye drove away.

Georgia turned to Emma, 'they're really nice aren't they, I've enjoyed this afternoon more than I expected to, I'm glad I came.'

'Good, I'm glad too. How are you settling into Godalming?'

'Oh, I love it here, Tom, he's my fiancé, he comes from here, we have one of those new flats on Chalk Road.' She checked her watch. 'He'll be waiting for me, it's my birthday today and we're going out to dinner. It was good to meet you Emma, I expect I'll see you again soon. Goodbye.'

Emma smiled at the young woman. 'Well, happy birthday Georgia. Goodbye.'

She watched until Georgia was lost in the crowd making for the gate. Then she picked up her bag and walked away.

Back in her flat Emma put the bag down on the small chest in the sitting room, she opened the top drawer and carefully removed the book and the photo frame from the bag, the frame went into the drawer then she wrapped her hands round the book and held it close for a long time before placing it on top of another identical volume and closing the drawer.

Emma sat in her armchair before opening the photo file on her phone. The one she had taken pleased her but the one Tessa had taken was the one that she would have printed up and fitted into the frame. It showed Emma with Jane on her left and Georgia to the right. Emma zoomed the shot and looked closely at the two women on the right. Despite the toll the years had taken on the one in the middle the similarity was clear, the same smile, the same calm grey eyes.

In the morning she would pack her bags and move on, somewhere, anywhere within commuting distance to London and far away from Godalming. She would find a hotel to stay in while she looked for another flat. Georgia wanted to set her free and so, naturally, she would go.

Godalming Events

Stuart 1603 – 1714
1698 – Peter the Great of Russia stayed at the King's Arms.
1682 – Framework knitting introduced to Godalming.

AN INTERVIEW WITH THE GODALMING GANG & THE INFAMOUS BANK ROBBERY OF 1966

by Martyn MacDonald-Adams

Scene: A living room in a small terraced house in Brighton Road, decorated in the classic style of the sixties – that is, cheap angular furniture covered with vinyl or other dubious plastics. It would originally have been excruciatingly colourful but thankfully it's all faded, worn and dusty now. The sky outside is grey.

Present are: -

JENNIFER: Jennifer Moore (JM), aged in her late sixties.

DAVID: David Moore (DM), aged in his mid-seventies and married to JM.

DERRICK: Derrick Berman (DB), aged well above seventy – a little senile. Mumbles a lot.

BARBARA: Barbara James (BJ) aged mid-twenties. She's interviewer from a local internet radio company. She's wearing a black top, close fit jeans and black ankle boots;

STEPHEN: Stephen Johnson (SJ) aged late twenties, BJ's assistant. He's a photographer, sound engineer, driver etc. He is wearing a suede jacket, white shirt, jeans and trainers.

Everyone is seated around the coffee table with Jennifer and David on the settee and everyone else on chairs. Barbara and Stephen sit together on one side. Stephen has headphones on and is looking at a laptop. There's a small microphone on a stand on the coffee table.

*****

BARBARA   <Into the microphone on the coffee table> Just a moment. Let me test the levels. Testing, testing, one, two, three…

JENNIFER   Take your time dear.

DERRICK   Should we really be doing this?

JENNIFER   Yes dear. I know what we're doing and we need the money.

STEPHEN   <Thumbs up and nods at BJ> Levels okay. Stand by for uploading... connecting… and we're... live! <Points to Barbara>

BARBARA   Hello. I'm Barbara James and I'm here at the home of Jennifer and David Moore and their long-time family friend, Derrick Berman. We're live streaming this interview for the very first time direct to you, our audience.

122

Jennifer and David, I'd just like to thank you for inviting us into your home. As you know we're here to interview you for our local radio channel, Surrey Hills Community Radio.

Now, you called us and said you have a confession to make? Tell us what you meant.

JENNIFER   How did you know?

BARBARA   Sorry? Know what?

JENNIFER   That we live here? We didn't tell anyone.

BARBARA   Oh, I'm sorry. I didn't mean… it was just a slip of the tongue.

DERRICK   It's my house it is. Mine.

BARBARA   Now, you and David are married and Derrick here is a long-time friend of both of you, is that right?

JENNIFER   Yes dear. A very, very close friend. He's been friends with us for, oh, I don't know, years and years. From the very start you might say.

DERRICK   <Mumbles> You wouldn't believe it's my house though.

BARBARA   Now, you claimed in your letter that you were the gang responsible for the Godalming High Street bank

123

	robbery in nineteen sixty-six. Is that right?
JENNIFER	Yes. That's right. We did that.
DAVID	Oh, it started before that.
BARBARA	Before what? The robbery?
DAVID	Oh yes. We tried to rob a train we did.
JENNIFER	David! There's no need to...
DERRICK	\<Mumbles\> They move in, take over. Derrick do this. Derrick do that.
DAVID	Didn't work though.
JENNIFER	Seriously David. There's no need to confess to *everything*.
DAVID	But we did try, though didn't we?
DERRICK	I can't even watch the TV like I used to.
JENNIFER	Maybe we did, maybe we didn't, but you nearly got Derrick killed both times.
DAVID	We needed the money!
JENNIFER	Actually Barbara, it started even before that. We needed a car. We were newly married then, without a penny to our name when clever clogs here, decides to buy one.
DAVID	That car was a bargain.

124

DERRICK   What car?

DAVID   Our first one. The grey Princess. Do
            you remember her?

DERRICK   Oh yes. Squeaky. That *was* a nice
            car.

JENNIFER   It was stolen.

DERRICK   It was a *nice* car.

DAVID   …and we needed it.

JENNIFER   Worse than that, it was stolen from
            the Johnsons up in North London.
            They had already used it for several
            post office robberies. Nasty lot the
            Johnsons.

DAVID   That's why Baldy Walder said it was
            such a good bargain.

DERRICK   It had leather seats.

JENNIFER   And where was Baldy when the
            police arrested you and confiscated
            it?

DERRICK   It had little silver handles to adjust
            them. Nice clean windows. The seats
            squeaked when you sat on them.

DAVID   It was a Vanden Plas Princess. It had
            a Rolls Royce engine. Only a few
            years old. Not much rust on it. It was
            a good car.

JENNIFER   Until the police took it away. Stupid

man!

DERRICK   Real leather. Squeak! Squeak!

BARBARA   What happened then?

JENNIFER   So, Billy Bright-Brains here,
               watches a western on TV and
               decides it would be a good idea to
               rob a train.

DAVID   It might have worked.

DERRICK   Squeak! Squeak! Squeak! David and
               Jennifer out in the car park again!
               Squeak! Squeak! Squeak!

JENNIFER   Derrick! Never mind him. He's gone
               senile.

DERRICK   Squeak! Squeak! Squeak! All the
               windows misted up…

DAVID   We wore out the leather on the back
               seats, didn't we Jen.

JENNIFER   I don't remember. Anyway… so
               these two reckon they'll rob the milk
               train. You know, the train that runs
               before the scheduled trains, by
               jumping off the bridge between
               Upper and Lower Manor Road.

DERRICK   It was two tone grey…

DAVID   It's a lot higher than you'd think.

JENNIFER   You bottled it, didn't you! You
               didn't jump in the end. Poor old

Derrick did though.

DAVID   Those trains were fast, you know?
             And it's a long drop from the bridge.

DERRICK   I went boinggg!

JENNIFER   Yes dear. At least you tried. You hit
             the roof and fell off. Broke a leg,
             didn't you.

DERRICK   Ouch! It hurt. Covered it in plaster.
             Then it itched.

DAVID   No money in milk trains anyway.
             Wasn't worth it. Next time we'll lay
             mattresses to either side in case
             Derrick falls off again.

JENNIFER   What do you mean 'next time'- you
             daft old coot! You're over seventy
             years old. *You* worry about breaking
             a bone every time you sneeze, let
             alone poor old Derrick here falling
             off trains!

DERRICK   Then there was Jonathon B. Squeak!
             Squeak! Squeak! Bounce! Bounce!
             Bounce!

DAVID   We couldn't afford train tickets in
             those days.

JENNIFER   And yet you *could* afford a stolen car
             - and those bungie cords.

DERRICK   Then there was Weasel Stephen.
             Squeak! Squeak! Squeak! Bounce!

Bounce! Bounce!

DAVID Those bungie cords nearly worked.

JENNIFER You were bouncing around under that bridge for nearly two hours. If the railway wasn't running a bus replacement service that day the police would have been in hospital with aching ribs - from laughing so much!

DERRICK <As if in throes of passion> 'Oh Jen.' – 'Oh Jen.' – 'Oh Jen.'

DAVID What's that Derrick?

JENNIFER Pay him no attention. He's having another one of his fits.

DERRICK You remember Weasel Stephen don't you Jen? I remember Weasel Stephen.

JENNIFER Do you Derrick? Do you really, 'Mister Senile'? You're the only one of us able to hide his own Easter eggs! Go take one of your pills.

DERRICK Squeak! Squeak! Squeak!

DAVID Is he trying to be a mouse?

JENNIFER He's in his fantasy universe again. Ignore him.

DERRICK Then there was Rotary Club. Squeak! Squeak!

JENNIFER	Derrick! Stop it! Where were we?
BARBARA	The bank robbery?
DERRICK	Squeak! Squea…
JENNIFER	<Angry> Stop it! Or no more hobnobs for you. Anyway Barbara, we did manage a nice holiday in Wales. Didn't we David?
DAVID	Yes. Abergavenny, Cardiff and Cardigan if I remember.
DERRICK	I never did get to bang 'er.
DAVID	I didn't know you wanted to go to Bangor?
DERRICK	Of course, I never told you though. She was married to you, wasn't she!
BARBARA	So, you tried robbing trains first?
JENNIFER	These two idiots did. It was then I realised that I had to organise them.
BARBARA	So, then you robbed the bank in Godalming High Street?
JENNIFER	Yes.
DAVID	It was my idea though.
BARBARA	So, *you* were the criminal mastermind?
JENNIFER	David? Ha!
DAVID	<Indignant> Criminal? No. No, I'm not a criminal.

JENNIFER   David couldn't mastermind his way
            into a little girl's Wendy House!

DAVID   She was mean!

JENNIFER   She was six years old.

DAVID   She stabbed me!

JENNIFER   With a plastic fork! Oh David, I wish
            you'd man up.

BARBARA   So, who… who planned the robbery?

JENNIFER   I did.

DAVID   With my ideas, I remember that. I
            have a photographic memory!

JENNIFER   Yes dear, but you're short sighted
            and have cataracts.

BARBARA   Tell me about it. What was the plan?

JENNIFER   We waited until it was about three
            o'clock in the morning. David
            managed to pick the lock on the back
            door while Derrick was on his step
            ladder dismantling the alarm bell. I
            held the sacks for the cash.

BARBARA   I thought it was a smash and grab
            raid?

JENNIFER   Yes, but it didn't start out that way.
            David set off the alarm just as
            Derrick had hold of the wires.
            Derrick got electrocuted, screamed
            and kicked the step ladder into the

back window.

DERRICK   But the alarm bells didn't go off.

JENNIFER   No dear, well done. You've never heard anyone scream so loud. Derrick nearly woke the entire town.

DERRICK   Electric shock. ZAP!!!

DAVID   I got in through the back window.

JENNIFER   Derrick fell and broke an ankle, didn't you Derrick?

DERRICK   I went boinggg!

JENNIFER   David opened the back door then I went in to help him.

BARBARA   That's when you unlocked the safe room?

JENNIFER   No. David had this special safe-burning powder didn't you David?

DAVID   It was my secret formula. My idea. Very cheap to make. I made it from my own formula you know.

DERRICK   …but my ankle went 'snap'. Ow!

JENNIFER   Except it wasn't safe was it, David?

DAVID   <Indignant> It's not my fault it caught fire.

BARBARA   So that's what caused the fire?

JENNIFER   Yes, but the fire brigade got there so quick, and they were so helpful.

Within minutes they burst in and asked us if we were alright.

DERRICK   Ouch! It hurt.

DAVID   That's when I had this bright idea. I shouted 'He's broken his ankle!'

JENNIFER   Yes, you pointed out the back window and the fireman thought you were pointing at the safe room. He opened the door for us. Then Derrick called for help and they all went outside to help him, leaving the door open for us.

DERRICK   Lots of big men in tall hats.

JENNIFER   We emptied out the safe room into the sacks then ran like bucks after a bunny... well, we ran away. The police arrived after that and arrested Derrick.

DERRICK   Lots of loud men in flat hats.

JENNIFER   But you didn't tell them about us, did you? You little angel. In the end the police thought he was just an innocent bystander who'd been attacked by the evil gang and we got away with it.

DERRICK   The firemen were no help. I described the Johnsons up in North London. The police thought it was them. Hee, hee!

132

DAVID	What was that?
DERRICK	I made the police believe it was the Johnsons from up in North London. I said one of them was called 'Baldy Walder'. Serve him right, selling us squeaky.
JENNIFER	You never told us that!
DERRICK	No. I can keep a secret I can.
DAVID	Not on a live radio interview you can't!
DERRICK	What do you... oh.
JENNIFER	Baldy is still out there! And now he knows!
DAVID	Oh no. Baldy... it was Derrick's fault; it was him who ratted.
BARBARA	...and this is Barbara James signing off from Surrey Hills Community Radio. I hope you enjoyed our little 'confession' today.
JENNIFER	Come here you senile ol' git! I'm gonna rip your...

<Sound stops suddenly>.

FINDING WITCHES

by Ian Honeysett

'Good evening Fellow-Godhelmians and welcome to our monthly gathering here at the White Hart Inn in Godalming High Street. This is our November 1585 meeting. By the way, in answer to a question, yes, it still is November. As I'm sure you know, the Gregorian Calendar was introduced in 1582 but it's only been adopted by Catholic countries like France and Spain. I doubt it will spread to England for well over a hundred years, so don't fret.'

'Now my name is Adrian Hanozet and I am your presenter this evening. As you know, we have to be out of here by 9.00pm – the closing time for hostelries such as this. So, without further ado, let us meet my guest for this evening, Mister Christian Caldwell.'

'Welcome, Mister Caldwell, or might I address you as Christian?'

'Good evening. No one should be reluctant to be addressed as a Christian, so please feel free to use my *Christian* name!'

'Well put, Christian. Now, please would you tell our audience here what your occupation is?'

'Of course. I am a Witch-finder.'

'Would you care to elucidate?'

'Indeed. Well, as you know, witchcraft, that foul heresy, has been with us for many centuries. Back in 1484, Pope Innocent VIII...'

'Wasn't he a Papist though?'

'Are you asking me if the Pope is a Catholic? Well, yes. But in 1582, of course, England passed the new Witchcraft Act so we now have firm legal grounds for Witch-finding.'

'And have you discovered many witches here in Godalming?'

'Oh yes. I'm afraid Surrey is by no means exempt from the evils of witchcraft. In fact, I was instrumental in exposing a coven of witches here in Godalming just recently. Probably the most infamous of them was Agnes Stevens, alias Waters. She had previously been accused of bewitching cattle belonging to Robert Bocher and Thomas Allen. Ten bullocks and a cow all died.'

'Bewitching cattle eh?'

'There's nothing amusing about it. No one wants a bewitched bullock! And she wasn't the only one. Three others were tried: Juliana Payge and Elizabeth and Joan Coxe: mother and daughter witches. They all pleaded not guilty but Agnes Stevens confessed.'

'And what was the outcome?'

'The three were found Not Guilty. But not Agnes.'

'So was she imprisoned or was she hanged? I understand that we don't burn convicted witches here in England?'

'No – just hanging. Far more civilised. But, in fact, neither fate befell Agnes as she was pardoned. A serious error which I argued against quite eloquently I thought.'

'Why do you call it an error?'

'Because the following year, she went on to bewitch humans. There were three victims: six-year-old Margaret Roker, Catherine Hammond and Richard Charman. She cast her spell on him on 21 June 1583 and he had a long, painful, lingering illness until his death on 20 July.'

'So can you explain the actual evidence that she was responsible for their deaths?'

'Ah, there was something of a problem there. As there often is in such cases. Witches are fiendishly clever. Nothing simple like a good, old-fashioned stabbing. But usually we have witnesses who are willing to testify that they saw or heard the witch do or say something witch-like.'

'Some argue that such 'witnesses' have other motives for making such accusations. Like money or revenge. Or just plain dislike.'

'Perhaps, in some cases, that is true. But we witch-finders have our own, proven tests. We look for the devil's mark for example. A spot on the skin which is dead to all feeling and doesn't bleed even when pricked.'

136

'Do you do the pricking yourself?'

'Good heavens, no, we employ specialised witch-prickers to do that! They are trained to look for hidden marks, perhaps a mole or a birthmark or an extra nipple. Sometimes these are well-hidden and they have to shave the accused of all body hair. Some believe that the witches' Familiars such as a dog or cat, will drink blood from those marks.'

'What happened to Agnes Stevens at this second trial?'

'Because she had previously pleaded guilty to being a witch, she was rightly convicted.'

'And was she hanged this time?'

'Alas no. She was merely imprisoned. Our legal system can be so lenient at times. They are rather more rigorous on the continent.'

'Perhaps if England ever joins more closely with the rest of Europe, we will have a more consistent approach?'

'Maybe but I cannot imagine that ever happening!'

'So are any convicted witches ever actually executed?'

'Oh yes, in another of my cases, Eden Worsley, a spinster of Ewell parish, was found guilty of murdering Elizabeth Bybye by witchcraft and sentenced to hang.'

'So it was *bybye* to Miss Eden then?'

'If that was an attempt at humour, Mr Hanozet, then I find it in extremely poor taste. There is nothing funny about witchcraft you know.'

'I apologise, Christian, I got a little carried away there. Do you see nothing at all *odd* about witch-finding? Only last year, Reginald Scot in his authoritative work *The Discoverie of Witchcraft*, wrote that those individuals who are accused of being witches tend to be 'old, lame, bleare-eyed, pale, fowle, poor, sullen, superstitious and papist'. What do you say to that?'

'There's some truth in it. On the other hand, that description does cover a great many people. I suspect that the devil selects those he feels most susceptible to his wiles.'

'And, rather unusually, the testimony of children is often admissible in witchcraft cases, isn't it, Christian? In Chelmsford back in 1566, I understand that three were charged with *acts of maleficium* ranging from tampering with livestock to harming infants and some of the key witnesses were children. I believe that in 1582 in St Osyth, 13 women were put on trial largely on the testimony of children?'

'Quite so – these are seen as exceptional crimes and so the evidence of innocent, undefiled, children is seen as appropriate. As the Good Book says: 'Unless you become like little children, you will never enter the Kingdom of Heaven'. After all, children can hardly be accused of having ulterior motives!'

138

'And spectral and ghostly evidence is also accepted. In fact, in the St Osyth trial, suspects didn't even need to be present when the alleged crime took place. Doesn't this make you feel a little *uneasy*?'

'There are many crimes where the suspect need not be physically present, Mister Hanozet. Poisoners for example. We are talking of spiritual crimes, after all, where malevolent spiritual forces are at work. So, no, this doesn't make me feel uneasy. I'm beginning to wonder whether you yourself are something of a sceptic in these matters? I hardly need remind you that our great Queen, Elizabeth, was fully supportive of the Witchcraft Act which made witchcraft illegal and subject to a civil rather than Church Court. So your levity in these matters might seem to some to smack not only of heresy but treason!'

'Now, please, Christian, I must protest. I was merely asking you questions that the Man in Godalming High Street might ask. So, one more question if you will: Why are witches always female and witch-finders always male?'

'An interesting but misguided question. I grant you that, in England, the majority of witches, perhaps three-quarters, are female but abroad this is by no means always so. In Russia, for example, the great majority are male.'

'And are there any female witch-finders?

'As far as I know, all are male. Just as all bishops are male. And lawyers. And...'

'Not so! Not so!'

139

'Who said that? Someone in the audience here? Identify yourself.'

'My name is John Hay from Moray in Scotland. I had never believed in coincidence until today. You see, I happen to be visiting a relative of mine who lives here in Godalming.'

'Welcome to our town, Mister Hay. So what is the *coincidenc*e you refer to?'

'Well, it so happens that a few years ago I was accused of witchcraft. Me, a Court Messenger! My accuser was a witch-pricker by the name of... Christian Caddell or Caldwell although, at that time, he went by the name of John Dickson. I was so outraged, I petitioned for his arrest. Although he disappeared, he was later caught and sent to trial and convicted of the grossest fraud.'

'Fascinating, Mister Hay, but what has it to do with our discussion this evening? Why did you say that not all witch-finders are male?'

'Because, Mister Hanozet, this witch-finder we have all been listening to this evening is that very witch-pricker, Christian Caldwell! And, at his trial, *he* was revealed to be a *she*! How she came to be here this evening is something of a mystery, I must confess, as she was sentenced to a lengthy period of imprisonment!'

'Christian, would you care to reply to these startling accusations? Christian? Christian? Where are you going? You can't just leave... Oh, you have.

And I haven't even paid you for being our guest this evening. Hold hard, where's my wallet gone?'

'Spirited away, I fear, Mister Hanozet!'

FOOTNOTE

There really was the witches' coven in Godalming in the 16th century and a case of a Witch-finder who was female but passed herself off as a man so she could pursue her profession. She, however, was not from Godalming!

Godalming Events

Edwardian 1901 -1914
1905 – Farncombe School opened.
1904 – Fire Station built in Queen Street.
1902 - Generating station built in Borough Road.

NOWHERE TO RUN
by Alan Barker

He put the bowl of food down and watched as Columbus hurtled in through the cat flap and set about his dinner.

William went into the bedroom and changed into vest, shorts and running shoes. As usual his clothes hung limply from his frame. The Pink Panther, Martha had called him.

Jogging in Broadwater Park was his favourite pastime, when he was able to rid his mind of all the dark thoughts. The steady pumping of his legs; the repetitive notes of song thrushes; the quiet concentration of anglers fishing for carp, all instilled in him a sense of contentment.

After completing his stretching exercises and taking a couple of deep breaths he strode along the hall, picking up a bottle of water on his way.

He passed through to the porch, the inner door swinging closed behind him.

*****

He gasped, swivelling round.

Too late.

He pressed his shoulder against the inner door; it wouldn't budge. More in hope than expectation, he tried the outer door but remembered locking it when he'd got home, as Martha had always encouraged him to. He patted his pockets but knew he'd left his keys inside.

With a stifled moan, he pushed open the letterbox and peered down the hallway. At the far end sat Columbus, licking his paws. William didn't have his mobile phone on him - he never took it on a run - but on a nearby table sat his keys, where he always kept them.

He straightened up and surveyed his surroundings. The porch was approximately eight feet square with a roof made of synthetic slate. Various tools and odds and ends were stacked in a corner and William rifled through them to see if there was anything he could use.

A long flimsy piece of timber seemed his only hope. Hunkering down, he fed the wood through the letterbox, angling it towards the table holding the keys. He found it difficult controlling the far end of the wood which quivered each time he eased it forward. But after much concentration, and with a gasp of triumph, he managed to poke it through the ring and lift the keys.

Suddenly Columbus, who had been watching with interest, leapt at the wood trying to grab it between his paws, succeeding only in dislodging the keys which skittered along the table and fell to the floor.

'What are you doing, you idiot cat?' William shouted.

Ignoring him, Columbus eyed the keys before prodding them further down the hallway, out of William's reach.

*****

'HELP!'

He had no idea how many times he had banged on the front door, sometimes merely in frustration rather than trying to attract attention. All he heard in response was the steady rumble of the Farncombe traffic.

Leaning against the door frame, he imagined himself jogging past The Cricketers, over the level crossing by Farncombe Station and along Summers Road before entering the park by Godalming Leisure Centre and setting off in a clockwise direction round the lake.

Eventually he sank to the floor, burying his face in his hands.

*****

Running on the spot.

One, two.

One, two.

One, two.

Keep those forearms driving but not too hard.

He could be in for the long haul. A marathon perhaps.

His passion for running seemed natural when he thought about it. Whenever he'd been naughty as a child his father had punished him by spanking his legs. One day he realised he could escape by dashing into the wood, and try as he might his father could never catch him.

He hadn't looked back since.

*****

One thing he was grateful for was that he had only intended having a salad for dinner. The consequences of leaving something cooking in the oven didn't bear thinking about.

He checked his watch: nine o'clock. Two and a half hours he'd been stuck in this prison.

How to get out? His door keys were still at the other end of the hallway, thanks to Columbus, and he didn't have his mobile to call for help. Worse still it was Friday evening, so he wouldn't be missed at work until Monday. He could hardly expect a spontaneous visit from his stand-offish parents despite the fact they lived just down the road in Binscombe, and his elderly neighbour wouldn't hear cymbals clashing in his ear. His only hope seemed to rest with someone delivering something the next day - the postman perhaps - but even then, William would have to direct him to where the spare key was hidden.

Had Martha not walked out on him she would be in the house and they would simply have laughed at his stupidity. The anguish he felt over losing her seemed exacerbated by his current predicament. He had always felt their relationship had been too good to be true, but what had prompted her to finish it? She'd insisted there was no one else but hadn't given any clear explanation for her decision. And trying to woo her back had been as unsuccessful as his attempts to get back indoors now.

How long could he survive with only the small bottle of water? At least he'd had the sense to restrict himself to a sip at a time.

He would need a pee at some point but it wasn't urgent - yet. He'd found a couple of old plant pots but they had holes in the bottom, so no luck there.

The biggest problem would be the cold. It was early April, three weeks before he was due to run in the London Marathon, so it could be worse. But wearing only a vest, shorts and running shoes he was clearly in for an uncomfortable night.

*****

Five o'clock in the morning. The only light penetrating the little porch came from a street lamp. He had slept sparingly, each time his awakening bringing a fresh bout of despair.

He sat with his back against the wall, an old doormat draped round his shoulders providing little comfort. He was shivering constantly.

Once again, he got up and banged on the outer door. A plaintive mewing came from inside the house - presumably Columbus expecting some food.

William flipped open the letterbox and peered through the darkness of the hallway. He could just make out the cat's pale-yellow eyes staring back at him.

Stalemate, William thought. I can't get back in and you're not getting any breakfast.

*****

As he dodged into the wood he glanced over his shoulder and saw his father in hot pursuit, a belt dangling from his hand.

His father's face was suffused with rage. Clearly he, William, had done something he shouldn't have but he couldn't for the life of him remember what.

He ran as fast as he could, nettles and brambles brushing his legs, but his father was gaining with every stride.

A tree root emerged from the darkness, sending him sprawling. He felt a hand swiping at his collar but wrenched himself free and set off again in a blind panic.

Shortly he realised he'd come full circle, their house looming up nearby.

He ran up to his bedroom, tears cascading down his cheeks, and locked the door behind him.

147

His heart racing, he listened as footsteps pounded up the stairs and stopped outside his room.

He backed away from the door, shaking uncontrollably, as a key turned in the lock.

*****

'What happened to you?'

William's eyes snapped open, but the harsh sunlight made him wince. Martha's willowy frame showed in the front doorway, arms folded across her chest.

'I shut myself in the porch last night,' he replied. 'I'm s-so glad you came.'

'This is only a flying visit, so don't get your hopes up. I thought I ought to bring this back.' Martha held up her key. 'And I might as well collect Columbus while I'm about it.'

'You're welcome to him.'

Martha paused and said, 'You look like a frozen scarecrow. Come on, I'll cook you some breakfast, try and put some meat on those skinny bones of yours.'

She held out her hand and he grasped it with as much strength as he could, desperately trying to hold back the tears.

NO WAY AT ALL

Poem by Pauline North

I'll do it my way or no way at all
And have no one near me when tears start to fall.
I'll raise up my chin and I'll paste on a smile,
All so they can't see my heart break all the while.

When well-meaning nurses smile softly, 'there, there.'
I'll shrug and say, 'oh well,' to show I don't care,
For it's only pain, by this name or another,
There's nothing you throw at me I cannot smother.

None of it's real of course, let me explain
I just won't let anyone look at my pain.
This is too private, I can't let them see,
I won't let a stranger get that close to me.

For sharing's for trusting and trusting is rare,
I can see in their faces they don't really care.
But my dear sweet husband, well he takes it all,
I seek his soft shoulder when tears start to fall.

REMEMBERING WITLEY & DISTRICT SOCIAL CLUB

by Christine Butler

As Leo entered the Witley surgery waiting room someone greeted him. 'Hello Father Christmas. I'm sorry I can't remember your real name. How are you?' The man smiled, thinking of the fun of those Christmas parties with excellent food, entertainment and presents.

Sitting down, Leo smiled back. 'At Witley Social Club. Of course. I'm afraid I can't remember your name either. But I'm used to still being called Father Christmas in the village, especially when my beard needs a trim. I played that part for a good many years.'

'White beard and bushy eyebrows,' observed the younger man. 'You only need the red coat and trousers now. Sorry, I'm being cheeky. Hey, Dad, get me out of a spot, will you? I may have put my foot in it.'

The door through to the surgeries had opened as someone came slowly into the waiting room. Ignoring his son, he exclaimed, 'Hello Leo. Fancy seeing you here.'

'Ted! How are you? Sorry, silly question,' Leo replied, 'In view of where we are'.

'What did the doctor say, Dad? Did he give you anything?' Ted's son Peter looked anxious as he helped his father to sit down.

'A different inhaler. And instructions to get more exercise. Can we walk down to The Star, son?' Turning to Leo again he added, 'Why don't you join us when you've finished here? I'd like to catch up on news. I don't get to Witley much these days, now I live in Bognor near my daughter.'

'Ok, but I don't promise. 'Bye for now. It's good to see you again.' Leo's name was called as the other two left.

*****

After his appointment with the doctor Leo 'phoned his wife, then drove his car the short distance to the Star car park. It was a long time since he had been in that pub for a drink. Ted and his son Peter were sitting in a corner of the main bar when he entered.

'Hello again,' said the younger man, standing up and coming forward. 'What would you like to drink?'

'Just a half of bitter, please. I'm not really allowed alcohol these days.'

'Nor's Dad. Sit down and I'll bring it to you.'

Leo crossed to the corner and joined Ted. After they had briefly compared notes on health problems and were starting on changes in the village Peter

151

returned with their beer, commenting, 'I thought I'd better stick to shandy as I'm driving,' as he carefully put the three glasses down.

'Thanks son,' Ted drank some of his beer, sighed contentedly and put the glass down. 'Now, Leo, what do you remember about the good times in Witley Club? When the beer was cheap and the club busy every weekend. We've been talking about it. But my memory's getting bad.'

'I remember the live music Saturday nights,' prompted Peter. 'All four of us used to go there – you, Mum, Maggie and me. Maggie used to dance and you and Mum complained that the music was too loud.'

'So did some of the neighbours. We had to keep the doors and windows shut.' Leo frowned.

'You were on the committee then, I think,' Ted commented. 'I was elected after you stood down, as I expect you remember.' He paused and took a swig of beer.

'Yes,' Leo agreed. 'After more than ten years I'd had enough. Too many arguments about finance. More could have been made of the upper games room to earn money,' he added. 'We had our silver wedding party up there. But it wasn't popular for that sort of thing 'cause of the stairs. And no upstairs loos.'

'We were all so much younger and fitter when that room was planned. No one thought of problems with stairs then,' mused Ted. Trouble was not enough youngsters became members. They'd come with their parents to the Saturday evening live gigs but drank elsewhere when they were older.'

'Some of them did join and played in the Village Games League.' Leo sighed. 'But I often had to 'phone round to get enough players each week when I ran the Witley team. You played darts for us; I remember.'

'Yes. Enjoyable evenings and visiting other clubs to compete. Snooker, shove-ha'penny, dominoes – that was your game wasn't it?' Ted smiled at Leo. 'And often you were driver for the team if it was an away match.'

'The League's just about running still,' Peter commented. 'I play darts sometimes for the club in Farncombe. But I'm afraid I go to my local pub when I want a beer, now I've moved back to Witley.' He paused for a mouthful of shandy. 'Did you go on the Rats' Outings, Leo?'

'Yes, I did. To Brighton by coach with a lunch stop on the way, then basically a pub crawl.'

'I remember Dad coming home rather the worse for wear. Did anyone ever get left behind in Brighton?'

'Only once. Someone missed him and shouted down the coach just after we left. The driver had to find somewhere to turn round and drove back along the prom. We spotted him crossing the road to get to the pick-up point outside the Aquarium, having forgotten the time.'

'Why 'Rats'?' Peter asked.

'From 'Rats' Corner' – the far end of the Club bar where their savings club to pay for the coach was based,' Ted contributed. 'I've heard that the Rats were started in the 1940s by a former steward, Les Cresswell, to help raise money for the Forces' Fund through various club events.'

'Do you remember the more recent charity evenings, raising money for the new GUTS charity at Guildford Hospital, Ted? Terry Scott used to come to give his support to the auctions held as he lived in the village,' said Leo. 'He swelled the number of people who came and did well for free drinks. It was good of him to give his time.'

'Guildford Undetected Tumour Scanning, or something like that. I remember the sponsored bed push for it. Hospital beds borrowed from Guildford Hospital and people dressed as nurses. When was that, Leo? It seems such a long time ago.'

'About 1985 I think,' Leo replied. 'Not so much traffic on the Petworth Road then. We had celebrity snooker and darts players visiting the Club too. I'm sure I remember John Lowe coming.'

'What happened? Why did the place go downhill?' Ted asked sadly. 'I know the Bowling Green was out of action for a while. That didn't help 'cause bowling was popular with members.'

'The damage caused by the gas pipe being repaired cost the Club a lot of money. The pipe went right across the centre so it had to be completely re-laid.'

'I remember that,' Ted replied, lost in thought for a moment. 'I suppose ageing or ill members had to stop coming and not enough new members joined.'

'Partly because beer prices went up. People drank elsewhere when the place started to look shabby and uninviting. Then it was a vicious circle.'

'Peter told me it closed in 2015. What's happening now? Will it be reopened?'

'I told you, Dad. They're building houses on the site and a small club room,' Peter replied for Leo.

'That's what we thought,' Leo explained. 'But when the Management Company that bailed us out put in the planning application it was turned down.'

'I'd like to go and have a last look at the place I spent so much time in,' Ted said thoughtfully. 'Is it still standing?'

'I haven't looked but I did hear that it's been knocked down following the sale. The new plans are for four semi-detached houses. The members voted against trying again for a small club room. It would have been something and nothing.'

'So, the old Witley Men's Club and Institute has gone completely, after more than ninety years. The village has lost another undervalued asset because the modern commuters now living here find their entertainment elsewhere.'

FOOTNOTE – WITLEY MEN'S CLUB & INSTITUTE

Witley had a Benefit Society and Institute in the 1800s for men and boys over 16 years of age. Local benefactor John Harrison Foster, a brother of the water colour artist Myles Birket Foster, had the Witley Institute clubhouse built in 1883-84. It was situated in Petworth Road not far from the White Hart and included a games room, reading room and library. It later became the Witley Royal British Legion clubhouse, then Foster's 1883 Club when the RBL club was closed.

The Institute moved to new premises in Mill Lane, built on land provided for a peppercorn rent by a local family. The first building was on what was later the car park, before the familiar red brick clubhouse replaced it. That was extended in 1972 and 1979. The club members purchased the freehold, probably in 1970 when it was incorporated, becoming Witley and District Men's Club and Institute Ltd. Women could only be associate members until the early 1980s when the name was changed again to Witley and District Social Club Ltd.

In recent years membership and therefore income reduced and the club room looked dated. There were financial problems, which meant there was no money available for modernising. Eventually on 22 October 2015 a meeting was held to inform the members that its future was bleak and the decision was made to close it. Plans were drawn up to demolish the building and replace it with 5 dwellings and a small clubhouse but these were refused by the planning department. A revised plan for four semi-detached houses and no club was accepted and the club was sold. These houses are now being built.

A SIMPLE MAN: LES CRESSWELL 1907 - 1986

by David Lowther

Many moons ago I was a teacher. One morning, my Headmaster commented that he felt society often undervalued ordinary folk: people who raised a family, did a constructive job for donkey's years and contributed towards the well-being of the community in which they lived.

Les Cresswell was such a person. Born in Suffolk in 1907, Les spent all but the first twenty-two years of his life in the villages of Milford and Witley, near Godalming. Before he died in 1986, Les sketched out his life in a fascinating memoir which his daughter Jenny was kind enough to let me read. He started working life as a poultry farmer, moved in that capacity to the neighbouring county of Norfolk before being offered a job in Milford.

A motor cycle journey from East Anglia to Surrey might seem an arduous trip, and indeed it was. Les got lost near London Bridge, somehow found his way to Elephant and Castle where he spotted a bus to Kingston which he followed to that town and from there he made his way to Milford. He lived in digs for a while. His enthusiastic comments about his landlady's rhubarb pie led to that pudding being served to him sixteen days on the trot.

Not that long after, Les was married to Hilda. They lived in a flat for a while then, after daughter Kathleen was born, moved to a small cottage where they secured a mortgage for the princely monthly sum of £2.11.11 (*in old money*). Life was hard and Hilda had to push the pram laden with baby and washing for a round trip of eight miles each Monday. A second daughter Jenny was born in 1935. Les meanwhile had moved to work in a sawmill where he could bolster his earnings through overtime.

In a life full of struggles and joy, Les and Hilda's life were blighted by tragedy. In 1939, Kathleen died of diphtheria. Not long afterwards, an accident at work left Les with a large part of his right hand missing. He was off work for more than six months and struggled on half pay. He returned to work as a paint sprayer but soon developed an industrial disease. The war was now on and, despite registering for the Navy, Les was, not surprisingly, found unfit for service. And so, in the middle of the conflict, Les became Steward of the Witley and District Social Club. There he remained for fourteen years, working hard at what was a very busy job; cleaning fires (4), chopping lighting wood, racking the beer and keeping it cool. He also had the unenviable task of restricting the members to two pints of ale a night in those ration restricted days.

Not perhaps part of his duties but, nevertheless, Les raised money from the club to send a pound a month to those members serving in the forces. Men away from their loved ones was but one of the aspects of the war that affected this part of the work. Guildford was bombed when Les was in hospital and a V1 landed in a field near Milford Junior School. Fortunately, there was little damage and no casualties. Hilda, meanwhile had given birth to two more children, Christine and Michael. She, like mothers the length and breadth of the land, had struggled during the war years with the effects of rationing and this continued with the severe austerity of the post-war period.

At the end of the war, Les organised a gala evening at the club which raised sufficient money to give each member returning from the services a wallet with £5 cash inside. He remained Steward until the mid-1950s and then worked for a local butcher for the rest of his life, first as a delivery van driver (he was affectionately known locally as the whistling roundsman) and, towards the end of his working life, in the shop. Even then, after a lifetime of family and community service, tragedy again stalked Les as he and Hilda lost their only son Michael in a motor cycle accident in Bermuda where he was working as a policeman. Two years later, Hilda died and her ashes, along with those of Kathleen and Michael, were buried at All Saints Church, Witley.

Les re-married in the mid-1970's. Mattie was his new bride. He died in 1986 and was mourned throughout the community, fondly remembered as a cheerful, generous man, popular with young and old and always whistling. Les and Hilda had four children of whom three survived into adulthood, and six grandchildren.

159

A life dedicated to family and community, he still had time to breed prize-winning rabbits. How many of us can say we have crammed as much into our lives as Les Cresswell?

FOOTNOTE

Thank you very much to Mrs Jenny Rawlinson, Les and Hilda's eldest surviving daughter for letting the author read the memoirs of Les Cresswell.

THE EYRIE
by Paul Rennie

Kenneth Higgins was the branch manager for *Homeward Property Services* in Mint Lane, an Estate Agency specializing in selling houses in Godalming and surrounding areas. Some people, rightly or wrongly, consider estate agents to be unscrupulous and shady, and Kenneth lived up to that reputation. Outwardly, he could come across as friendly and personable, although that persona quickly vanished as soon as he received his fees. He thought nothing of overvaluing properties to get contracts with sellers, charging excess commissions, and then encouraging them to drop the price below the market value 'because he had a cash buyer lined up'.

He was a master of the art of gazumping, playing off one buyer against another, or introducing fictitious rival bids, usually in the final stages of a sale when buyers are at their most vulnerable, to maximize his commission. His forte, though, was property description. His brochure details were masterpieces in half-truths and whole lies. No matter how run-down or badly situated a house was, he could make it sound like it was the most desirable property in the area. Problems like rising damp became a positive because the wall above must be so dry because the roof was good. Draughts and ill-fitting windows meant good ventilation. Close proximity to pylons and phone masts meant that there was a good electricity supply and mobile signal.

There was nothing he couldn't put a positive spin on. He prided himself on his wide-angle lens camera, which could make a cupboard look like a baronial hall. He had an elastic tape measure that could stretch into the deepest recesses of room to make them sound bigger than they were. Box bedrooms became huge double rooms, an entrance hall would become an extra reception room, and the smallest galley kitchen became a space you could entertain in. In short, there was nothing he wouldn't do to get a sale and make his commission, and what he lacked in honesty and integrity he made up for with ambition and perseverance. He was so successful at this, that he had twice achieved branch manager of the year, and had a tidy sum of money in his bank account, a sum sufficient for him to consider entering the property market himself.

Just around the corner from his rented flat, there was a rather run down Victorian house, called *The Eyrie*, perched on the side of Frith Hill, a steep sandstone slope with beautiful views over the town and Wey Valley. It was owned by a lady called Mrs Pritchard who was in advanced years and lived on her own in the rambling house. Kenneth was looking out for just this opportunity. He started by hand delivering flyers through her letter box, stating that there were cash buyers looking for houses like hers in the area, and offering a free valuation. In this particular case, he was careful not to use *Homeward Property Services* stationery, as he coveted this house for himself. He could see it had huge potential, and hoped the owner didn't realize this.

Eventually, he got a call on the private phone number he had used, from a very frail and confused sounding lady who asked him what the leaflet was about. He talked her into inviting him round to give a valuation. That evening, he stood on her doorstep, and rang the doorbell. There was an eternity before a small figure shuffled its way to the door and fumbled with the lock, finally opening it a fraction and peering myopically out at the tall man wearing a slightly shiny pinstripe suit and a beaming smile. 'Good evening Mrs Pritchard, I'm Ken Higgins from *Homeward.*'

The old lady gave him a blank look.

'We spoke on the phone, Mrs Pritchard. I'm here to give you a valuation on your house.'

'Pardon,' she said, 'could you say that again, only my hearing isn't what it was.'

'I'm Ken from *Homeward Property Services*, and you asked me to come round and give you a valuation.'

'Oh yes, valuation, that was it. Who did you say you were again?'

'Ken Higgins.'

'Would you like a cup of tea, only I don't get many visitors and I've no family.'

'No thanks,' said Ken, inwardly rubbing his hands together. No friends, no family, no one interfering. She was going to be a pushover.

'This must have been a lovely house, but I can tell it's seen better days, and I bet it costs a fortune to run.' He cast his eye round the room cluttered with objects and photos from a bygone era.

'It must be very difficult to look after, and those stairs look like a death trap. If you were to stay here it would take a huge amount of money to make it safe and comfortable.'

'Yes', she said, 'I have days when I get terribly confused and can't remember where I left my slippers. If they are upstairs I have to go up on my bottom and down on my hands and knees.'

'Don't you mean, up on your hands and knees and down on your bottom?'

'That's right, bottom,' said Mrs Pritchard.

He noticed she was wearing her cardigan inside out, and her socks didn't match. Clearly she was suffering from advanced dementia. He mentally took a few more thousand off the price he was hoping to pay.

'Well perhaps I could take a look around and get a feel for the market value.'

'Yes,' said Mrs Pritchard, 'While you're doing that I'll get you that cup of tea you asked for.'

Ken wandered around the house looking in the dusty rooms, but he didn't write down any details or take any measurements. None of those were going to appear in *Homeward Property Services's* glossy brochure. It was the view out of the back rooms that he was most interested in. As he expected, it was magnificent. The small garden sloped downwards for about 20 yards, to the rear boundary, and then the ground dropped vertically more than 50 feet to the house below. There was an uninterrupted 180 degree view over the town and the Lammas lands to the river Wey, and beyond that the green hills of Unstead. It was priceless, but he was certainly going to come up with one, and a low one at that. He would demolish the old house and build a smart new home with large windows and a balcony to make the most of the views.

*****

He went back downstairs. The kettle was boiling dry, and Mrs Pritchard had fallen asleep in the armchair. He turned off the gas, and then tapped her on the arm. 'Hello Mrs Pritchard.'

'Who are you?' she asked.

'I'm Ken, the estate agent. I'm here to help you sell your house.'

'Oh, yes' she said, 'Would you like another cup of tea?'

'Oh no thank you,' said Ken 'One is enough for me, I have to watch my waistline. Now I've had a look round, and we would be prepared to take this house on. Unfortunately, the market is very slow at the moment and houses like this are very difficult to sell. It would take thousands of pounds to make it safe and suitable for a family to live in. I'm afraid we would need to price it quite low, otherwise you could be stuck with it for years waiting for a buyer. I think the maximum you could ask for it is £120,000, but be prepared to accept offers. Fortunately, I have a lovely family on my books, who can't afford much, but would be prepared to live in a house in this condition. What do you think?'

'Well,' said Mrs Pritchard 'I'd like it to go to a nice family who would keep it like it is and not change it. There are a lot of memories in this house, even though I've forgotten most of them.'

Ken had a mental image of the bulldozers surrounded by rubble.

'Of course,' he said, 'The Johnsons are an old-fashioned family who don't go in for modern stuff. They would keep it exactly as it is. Maybe you could visit from time to time, they'd love that.'

'That's nice' said Mrs Pritchard, 'I'd like that.'

'I'll give the Johnsons a call,' said Ken, 'and see what we can do.'

He dialled his own office number. 'Hello Mr Johnson, I've found a house that you might like, owned by a lovely lady, Mrs Pritchard. I know you'd like her. She is keen to sell her detached house on Frith Hill. It's called *The Eyrie*, and she is after £120,000. Oh, you know it? You'd like to put in an offer sight unseen. Ok, I'll tell her the good news.'

'Well,' he said, 'Very good news indeed. They would be prepared to offer £100,000 in cash.'

Mrs Pritchard looked alarmed. 'I'd need to think about it. Maybe I'll ask the Postman what he thinks'.

Ken was determined to keep the Postman out of it. 'I tell you what, Mrs Pritchard, or can I call you Elsie? I'll call the Johnsons again and tell them that you want to hold out for the asking price.' He called his office number again, and explained Mrs Pritchard's concerns to the voicemail. 'Oh, to help her, you'd pay the full asking price. That's very generous, Mr Johnson. I'll let her know.'

He explained to Mrs Pritchard that they were prepared to pay the £120,000 asking price.

'Thank you,' said Mrs Pritchard, 'I'm sure the Postman will approve when I tell him.'

'Oh, I wouldn't bother him, Mrs Pritchard, I'm sure he's a very busy man. Anyway, you need to decide quickly. This week at *Homeward*, we are offering zero commission in what we call Goodwill week. It runs out tomorrow. So today I can sell the house for free, whereas next week, I'm afraid, I would have to charge you our standard 4% rate, which would be thousands of pounds. You have to be quick in this business. If it were up to me I would give you more time to decide, but it's Corporate policy.'

'That's very nice of you,' said Mrs Pritchard, 'I need to get as much as possible to pay for my care home. *Sunset Endings* charge extra for people in my condition, and the money in my teapot wouldn't cover it.'

'I tell you what, I'll give them another call and say you're worried about the care home, and see what we can do.' He dialled his office number again, 'Hello again Mr Johnson, Mrs Pritchard is a bit concerned about her care home fees, is there any way you could improve your offer. You would, you'd go up to £140,000? Ok, I'll run it by her.'

'Fantastic news, Elsie. I've persuaded them to offer £140,000. That's more than the asking price. That doesn't happen very often, I can tell you. We could get the ball rolling tomorrow if you accept, and you could be in your nice warm safe care home and away from this damp cold draughty house in a month. Wouldn't that be nice?'

Mrs Pritchard was still unsure. 'I've just planted some new bulbs in the garden and was hoping to see them come up.'

'I could have another word with the Johnsons, although they might be putting the children to bed by now. Suppose I can get them to pay a little more, so you could afford a room at *Sunset Endings* with a view of the garden? That would be nice wouldn't it? I'm sure they would let you plant some bulbs and you could watch them come up in spring.'

'If you stick around that long', he thought unkindly.

'Hello again Mr Johnson, sorry to bother you again. Can I hear your children crying in the background? Yes, it must be so difficult with five of you in the same room. I know your situation is desperate, but could you up your offer to £160,000, and I'm sure Mrs Pritchard would accept that. Oh good, you will if you can move in the next month, thank you'.

'There you go, Elsie. Who dares wins eh? £160,000. What a result! They did agree, provided it is a quick sale, as they are living in Bed & Breakfast at the moment with their three young children, and are desperate for a proper house. I could hear the baby coughing because of the damp conditions.'

'Oh dear, I'm all in a fluster,' said Mrs Pritchard, 'Those poor children. I'd like to help them, but I'm wondering what my husband Alf would have thought. He loved this house. Would you like that cup of tea now?'

'No thank you. I tell you what, I'll have one last try and see what we can do.' He dialled again.

'Mrs Pritchard is worried what her late husband would think if she was selling the house with all of her memories of him. I see, you understand. You'd raise your offer to £180,000 and she could come round and stay here anytime she wanted. You'd even keep her bedroom untouched with her belongings in it, so she could stay in it. Oh that is a lovely idea. I'll tell her.'

Mrs Pritchard appeared to have fallen asleep again, so he woke her and explained the latest offer and arrangements. She smiled and said that was nice, and then said she needed to go to the loo because all that tea had gone through her.

After another eternity she doddered back. 'Now what were we talking about?' she said brightly.

'I was explaining that Mr and Mrs Johnson are prepared to offer you well over the market value of the house and let you come and stay in your old room as often as you'd like, but they need an answer today because they've just seen another house in the area for a lower price and they are thinking of going for it.' Ken was losing his patience and was exhausting his repertoire of tricks to get a sale. 'As your agent and friend, I strongly recommend that you take this deal. This is a once in a lifetime offer.'

Mrs Pritchard smiled. 'Has that kettle boiled yet?'

'I'll go and check,' said Ken, 'and give you time to think.' He went to the kitchen at the back of the house. The view was stunning. He could imagine himself having breakfast looking out through panoramic windows. He just had to have it. He just had to persuade the old bat to part with it.

He went back into the sitting room and woke Mrs Pritchard up again. 'Here's a nice cup of tea, have you decided yet?' He explained the arrangements to her again.

'Oh dear,' said Mrs Pritchard, 'I'd forgotten about the moving costs and how I would get back here from the care home, and what about poor Kitty? Who would look after her?'

Ken was starting to get exasperated. 'I'll see what we can do about the costs and how to look after

Kitty.' He dialled his office number again, with its almost full voicemail box.

'Mr Johnson, Mrs Pritchard is almost there. We just need to find a way to cover her moving and travel expenses, and sort out someone to look after her cat. Suppose you raised your final offer to a nice round figure of £200,000? That would cover Mrs Pritchard's moving expenses and taxi fares. Yes, you would? Thank you, and you love cats so you would be happy to look after Kitty? That's very kind of you.'

'Wonderful news, Elsie. The Johnsons have always wanted a cat and would be delighted to let Kitty stay here with them so that she didn't have the stress of a move.'

'As soon as the move's complete, Kitty's going on a one way trip to the vets,' he thought to himself.

'And, Elsie, they will pay you £200,000, which is double what we thought we would get for the house, and that would cover all of your expenses.'

'Oh dear it's all happening so quickly. Maybe I should think about it and let you know tomorrow.'

Ken threw his final gambit. 'I tell you what, Elsie, you are such a lovely lady, and because we are such good friends, I'm going to help you out with my own money. The Johnsons can't afford any more, but I will top up their offer with £20,000 of my own money, because I just want what's best for you. It was money I was saving for an operation, but you are such a lovely lady, I want you to be happy. In fact, I

171

like your company so much, that I will pick you up from *Sunset Endings* and drive you here myself any time you want. All you have to do is call.'

'That's lovely, dear,' said Mrs Pritchard, 'How much does that make it? I've already forgotten.'

'You would get £220,000 in cash, and you wouldn't have to worry about getting a solicitor, because I have a friend who will help you out for no charge.'

'In that case, since you are such a nice young man who has been so helpful, I'll take the offer.'

'Very good, Elsie. You have made a wise decision and you won't regret it.'

'Not half you won't,' he thought, gleefully. 'Now if you would just sign this contract agreeing to start proceedings and engaging my services, I'll do all the rest.'

Mrs Pritchard peered at the contract sheet that he had filled in with the £220,000 figure. After a few minutes she realized she had the wrong glasses on, and fumbled for another pair with extra thick lenses that made her look owl-like. Eventually, she took the pen that he proffered, and, after an attempt to use it upside down, finally managed to scrawl a spidery signature almost on the line he had shown her.

After the formalities, he said goodnight and walked back to his flat. He had paid more than double what he had hoped to get the house for, but once demolished, and a new house with that view, he would make a fortune.

One month later, and with the £220,000 transferred to Mrs Pritchard's bank account, the sale was completed. He now had the deeds to the house, and Mrs Pritchard had moved out. He was expecting her to call him for lifts or visits, but strangely, there was nothing. 'That's good,' he thought, 'It saves me having to make up excuses.' There was also no sign of the cat. 'Great,' he thought, 'Hopefully it's been run over.'

He hadn't bothered with a survey of the house, nor did he take out insurance. What was the point, when he was going to demolish the house anyway? The view was all that mattered.

That summer had been exceptionally dry, and the Surrey Hills area had had its lowest rainfall since the drought of 1976. The ground had become extremely parched, and deep cracks had appeared in the soil where the moisture had evaporated. Then, at the end of that week in October, the weather broke and there was torrential rain for days on end. The water soaked back into the ground through the cracks. It reached the subsoil, turning it into a slurry.

On the night of the 9th, after a further day's rain, the ground that *The Eyrie* was perched on started to slip. First there was a slight shivering, and then trees around the property started to lean down the slope. The rear lawn rippled in corrugations and, with the flowerbeds, slid towards the back fence, which opened like a drawbridge to let the mass of debris through to tumble down the cliff. Then, the whole house started to move, following the rear

173

garden down to the boundary. It hesitated at the top of the cliff, then slowly tilted and toppled over into the garden of the neighbour below. It was joined by the front garden right up to the road boundary. Even the foundations tumbled down. When the landslip finally stopped, nothing remained of the house and garden. There was just a neat edge of tarmac at the road, a gap where once the house had stood, and a few pipes and wires sticking out of the ground.

*****

When Ken strolled round to view his newly purchased property, he was met by the astonishing sight. He stood there aghast. At first, he thought he was in the wrong place, except there was *The Eyrie* signpost written in gothic script. Where the house had stood on its plateau set into the hillside, there was nothing except a sandy slope, far too steep and unstable to build a house on. As he stood on the road looking in dismay, the signpost tipped over, skittered down the slope and disappeared over the edge like an Olympic ski jumper. Every so often a few more stones and rocks rolled down the slope and dropped over the edge. The view was still there, if anything even more magnificent, but that was all. He had lost everything. But, it was even worse than that. Next day he got a letter from the owners of the house below, asking for details of his insurance company, as he was liable for clearing away the debris that had fallen into their garden.

Mrs Pritchard sat in the comfortable chair in the house she now shared with her sister. She put aside the Times crossword that she had just completed and reached for her iPad to check her investment portfolio. She decided that she had made enough to go ahead and book the Caribbean cruise she had promised the two of them. She glanced at the coffee table next to her, where she could see the *Surrey Advertiser* with its headline describing the unfortunate landslide that had occurred on Frith Hill. Next to it was a Structural Engineer's report from earlier that year, warning that *The Eyrie* was in a precarious state from subsidence, and needing remedial work costing millions.

She allowed herself a little smile, opened the iPad browser and typed in: www.p&ocruises.com.

NEW WORLD

by Pauline North

The young male stirred, reluctant to abandon his sleep, his pale grey eyes opened and slowly focussed. Kite yawned and stretched before pushing off the cover and climbing out of his sleep station. He pulled out the earbud, placed it carefully back in its box then he shook his head slightly to clear the residual hum. During the day he would return the bud to the education room and collect the next night's lesson.

Still yawning he walked into his tiny shower room. A few minutes later back out and wrapped in a towel, he checked the day's schedule on his screen. Then dried himself and dragged on some clothes.

'What's the time, slave?'

The information slave lit up blue. 'In fifty seconds the door will unlock for the feeding hour.'

'Thank you slave.' The blue light faded.

Kite picked up his warming shirt – outside of the rooms the passageways, tunnels of bare concrete, were always bitterly cold – and slipped it on as he moved to the door. The door clicked open and he moved out and joined the other young males with rooms on the same floor. They shuffled along in silence, not too fast. Moving too fast or communicating was forbidden in the passageways because that used too much energy and the collectors

176

imbedded in the ceiling harvested excess energy and used it to light their way.

Once they reached the eating place and had been allocated their morning nourishment they gathered in groups, seating themselves round the tables.

For whole minutes the only sound was the faint slurp of the semi liquid food as the young males spooned it up as fast as possible. When the last dish was empty then was the time for conversation.

Lute leaned close to Kite, 'Did you see the females as we passed the door to their eating place?'

There were surreptitious glances to see if anyone was listening. Lute said, 'Luna was standing by the doorway, I swear she looked at me.'

There were snorts of disbelief. 'Of course she didn't,' Dune cut in, 'we're too young, she will have to choose one of the young matures.'

'Well I have been working it out,' said Kite, 'I think we may soon be declared young matures.' He spoke quietly, nodding to make it definite.

The heads closed together to keep others from hearing. 'You mean that then the females could come and pick one of us?' Lute breathed the question, his eyes darting all round.

There was no more time to talk, the voice of authority, the Master, boomed out, silencing all the young males.

'Attention, I have information. This evening, beginning at the ninth time sector, six young males will be notified that it is time for their transformation,' there was a dramatic pause. 'Then you will be escorted to new rooms in the young mature building. You may now all go to your morning work, attend your group studies as usual this afternoon then at the end of the day you will return to your rooms and wait.'

In the crush at the doorway shocked young faces, a little pale, looked into the faces of their companions, eyes asking questions they dared not voice.

Kite was allocated to the packing floor where he spent the morning packing small super-electronic items into boxes and stacking them for the bots to take to distribution; he passed away the hours wondering if he would be among the young males judged ready to take the step to young mature, perhaps then he would be given work that was more interesting.

The afternoon study session was one of the few occasions when young males and females were in the same place at the same time, although they were segregated with females on the left side and males to the right.

That afternoon the study subject was the effect on the ecology of the universal policy of imposed veganism. A short discussion compared the benefits of arable farming compared to animal husbandry. Kite paid very little attention until a livestock farm was shown on the large screen; he was surprised to see the care shown to the animals. Kite had never seen images of cows and sheep before and found them appealing. He particularly liked the cows, large curious creatures with gentle eyes.

When the cameras moved to show endless fields of cabbages he turned away from the screen, disappointed. Luna was watching him, paying sharp attention. He flushed slightly and looked away. The afternoon's lesson ended with the conclusion that although people used to eat animals, as the world changed enlightenment led the people to reject such barbaric behaviour, to the benefit of both humans and the natural world.

As soon as he reached his own room that evening and the door closed behind him Kite sat on his sleep station to gather his thoughts, if he was chosen to be transformed that was a good thing, surely. His thoughts turned to Luna, if he was to be chosen by any of the females he hoped it could be her but then how much chance did he have? All the young males cast their eyes towards her, Luna, with the pale hair and that disconcerting way she had of almost smiling at you before she turned away.

He stood and looked into the mirror. At almost eighteen, only medium height with a slight build and floppy brown hair why would she choose him, he told himself to put those thoughts away and forget them.

For a while Kite waited for the knock on his door that would be the Master, come to select him, then he curled up on his sleep station convinced that he would be passed over, he had been judged unsuitable.

When the knock came Kite was so wrapped in self-pity that it took him a moment to realise what he had heard, he quickly crossed to the door and opened it. The Master strode into the room bringing with him the aura of power.

'Kite,' he always presented his words as if each one was precious. 'I have pleasure in transforming you from a young male to a young mature. This comes with all the benefits of added status, a move to a larger room in the young mature building and of course you will be allowed to mate with a female, should any of them select you. Do you understand?'

'Yes Sir – Master, thank you.'

'Collect together your belongings. A bot will be along soon to escort you to your new room.'

The Master swept out, the tails of his cloak fluttering behind him.

Kite stared at the empty doorway. Slowly he sat on the edge of his sleep station, no not his sleep station any more, he had to be ready to move. A quick dash round the room that had been his only home and Kite stuffed his lifetime of possessions into a single bag.

When the bot arrived Kite walked out of his room without looking back. With his bag slung over a shoulder he followed along bare passages, out of the building and across the vast exercise yard to the building where the young matures and the females lived. He followed the bot down a long passage, gazing in wonder at the bright lights and the painted walls. He was shown to his room, the door opened and he was left alone.

Kite examined his new room, it was only a little larger than the one that had been his home all of his life. He sat in the chair in front of his new screen, nothing had really changed, the new walls still confined him just as the old ones had. He felt lost and alone.

Slowly he became aware of, not a sound as such, more a change in the quality of the silence outside his door. He told himself to ignore his stupid imagination, then, curious, Kite crossed to the door and opened it a crack.

The lights in the passage had been dimmed but in the deepest shadow, close to the wall, he saw Luna, he opened his mouth to speak but she put a finger to her lips and slipped into the room.

'Close the door, quickly.'

'What are you doing here?'

'I think we must talk, Kite.'

Kite stared at her, he knew the females were free to choose their mating partners but this wasn't how he had imagined it would be

'Um, talk, yes we could talk first, if you like.'

A sudden vivid smile lit Luna's face. 'No, not that, well not at the moment anyway.'

181

Kite turned away to hide his scarlet face. 'Why then?'

'I've been watching you, I saw your face when the tutor showed those animals, now I know that you are the one I want to come with me.'

Kite sat on the edge of his sleep station. 'Explain please.'

'You were born here?' he nodded. 'I was brought in, as a small child. They tried to erase my memory but they failed, I still remember, I know about outside.'

'There are other places like this, I do know that.'

'No, well there are but there is free country too, places they haven't made like this, where you can still see the sky, where there are fields and roads and people still live free. I want to go back, will you help me?'

'They won't let us out, only the convoys go and they can only go with guards. Are you sure about the fields and anyway how could we get out?' then as an afterthought, 'If I come with you can I see the animals? I really liked the cows.'

Luna reached and took his hand, 'No, sorry Kite, there aren't any now, all the land was needed to grow crops,' she looked away with tears in her eyes. 'They all had to be slaughtered.'

They were silent for a moment then Luna pulled his hand to get his attention. 'They call this complex Godalming don't they?'

'Yes this is Godalming.'

'There is a real Godalming out there, a small town that has been in its place beside a river for longer than people remember. It's a shadow of the place it was but we could gather together others like us and make it a home. Once we get away they won't bother with us, not now, they are too busy trying to keep this failing experiment going.'

Hopes and dreams took fire in Kite's mind, 'but how do we get out, Luna?'

Slowly Luna took a small box from her dungaree pocket. 'I have been working on this, testing it, it works. I can unlock any door with this.'

Without another word Kite picked up his bag, the two young people slipped out of the room and along the dim passageways. They crept like wraiths through doors and across courtyards until they reached the containing barrier and an exit. The first light of a new day glowed through the opaque door.

Luna held the box against the lock, grinned at Kite and pressed a button. There was a click. Hardly daring to try, Kite took hold of the handle, it slid open easily. They were through in a second closing and locking the door behind them. Luna took Kite's hand and as the new day's sun rose into a clear blue sky they walked through long, dew soaked grass towards the distant town of Godalming that sheltered down by a shining river.

Godalming Events

Norman 1066 – 1154
1086 – First mention of Compton, Farncombe, Hambledon, Hurtmore, Littelton, Loseley, Peper Harrow, Rodsell, Tuesley and Witley Manors (all split from the original Godalming Manor) in Domesday Book.
1066 – Godalming held by William I after the Norman Conquest.

LOVER'S LAMENT

Poem by Julie Buckingham

In dawn's early light, so bright,
I take you to a place of beauty
in the Surrey countryside,
where you can rest lightly,
shielding your closed eyes
from the sun,
which you will see no more.

For the devil in me,
took me by surprise...
by sunrise
you were dead in my arms.

I – the country bumpkin
your father hated so much,
had strangled you
until you were blue-veined and lifeless,
until there was nary a sound,
from your mouth so round,
only stillness.

And the clock ticked
its minutes away,
into this new year,
annoying me
so that I knew I had to move fast
to take you here at last –
to the place where you and I

185

first met.

With trembling hands
I lay you to rest
in quiet solitude,
your scolding tongue, at last,
no more.

For myself, I give not a care
for I know they will hang me,
(when they find me),
sometime in this year
of eighteen ninety four.

HUMPHREY, JEFFREY & GODFREY: THE INHERITANCE

by Martyn MacDonald-Adams

Early next morning there was a knock on the front door.

'They're here!' yelled Humphrey from the kitchen as he removed his pink floral pinafore.

There was a rumble along the hallway and a 'Boink!' sound as Godfrey dashed out of his room, faster than his legs could cope, bumped into the front door and hurtled backwards to land flat on his back.

'Ow!' he said, rubbing his nose.

'So now we know. Little bears' noses are *very* bouncy,' said Humphrey. He glanced down the hall to see Jeffrey dragging himself reluctantly toward them.

'But I suspect we'll have much longer to wait to find out if larger ones are just as squishable.'

Humphrey pulled open the front door.

'Hello. Humphrey?'

In front of him stood three female bears, in descending order of height; Bernadette, Colette and little Yvette.

'Hello Bernadette. Girls,' replied Humphrey. 'We've been expecting you. Do come in.' The girls entered the gang's home and took off their damp coats (it was raining outside). Humphrey passed them over to Godfrey. As he showed the girls into the living room Godfrey staggered back towards his bedroom but didn't make it, falling over and dumping their wet clothes on the floor. As it happens this was a good thing because the hall was in need of a clean.

In the living room Humphrey tried his best at being sociable but sadly, this is not one of Humphrey's best skills. Fortunately, he'd prepared for their arrival and had a list of subjects memorised.

'Please, ladies. Take a seat. You must be Colette and Yvette. Did you have a nice journey? I do like your dress. Can I get you a cup of tea? How are you keeping? What pretty earrings. Have you had your holidays yet? Are you warm enough? It's been such a long time. Would you like some biscuits? Isn't the weather just appropriate, or not? Should I turn up the heating? How is Aunty Florrie? Would you prefer milk or orange juice? Let me turn up the heating.'

Humphrey, having now exhausted all his ice-breakers in less than fifteen seconds, ran out the room to turn up the heating. He congratulated himself on remembering them all. Yay!

Godfrey dodged the triumphant bear as he flew past, and peered round the living room door.

'Hullo,' he said.

'Hullo,' said little Yvette. The smallest of the three.

'I've got a colouring book,' said Godfrey, who then turned around and left. Yvette, without any prompting, got down from the chair and followed him to his room. Within just a few seconds they had both settled down and were colouring in scenes of animals in the woods, marine creatures in the sea and birds pooing on the cars parked in Godalming's various Town Centre car parks.

At their age, six words are enough. A skill completely lost on human politicians.

Jeffrey hung about outside the door wondering what to do, what to say and how to say it when Humphrey arrived with a tray of several cups and saucers, a tea pot, a sugar bowl and some biscuits.

'Come on in and say hello,' said Humphrey.

'Do I have to?'

'Yes. They're your cousins. They've come to visit us for the day. You have to say hello. There are rules.'

'Can't you say it for me?'

'Oh, for goodness sake! Open the door and go in.'

Humphrey followed Jeffrey into the living room and placed the tea tray on the coffee table. He stopped and thought for a moment. 'Is it right to put tea on a coffee table? It seems wrong somehow.'

'Perfectly all right.' Bernadette smiled. 'And to answer your questions... yes, yes and yes. Thank you. That would be nice. Fine. Thank you. No. Yes, thank

189

you. Indeed. The girls might enjoy them. Isn't it? There's no need and she's fine. The girls might prefer them and really, there is no need.'

Humphrey was now aware that the entire morning's conversation had just been comprehensively completed in just a few minutes, but he took solace in the thought that having muffed up the first round, they could start again from the top and this would fill in even *more* time. So, in point of fact, this had proved to be a brilliant conversational tactic. He made a mental note for next time.

'Here is Jeffrey. Say hello Jeffrey.'

'Hello Jeffrey,' mumbled Jeffrey staring down at the carpet.

'We seem to be missing some bears.'

Bernadette smiled. 'Godfrey and Yvette have already made friends and have gone to play.' She turned to Jeffrey. 'My, my. How you've grown. You're a big handsome bear now. Perhaps you'd like to show Collie around?'

Jeffrey perked up. There was a dog here? Where? Then he realised Bernadette was referring to Colette and his face dropped.

'Uh.'

Humphrey stepped up. 'Show Colette your laboratory and workshops. I'm sure she'd be interested in your nuclear powered, bungee assisted, high altitude sandwich delivery device.'

'Uh. It's supposed to be a secret.'

'That's alright Jeffrey. We're all family here. Besides, it's a good idea.' Humphrey turned to Bernadette. 'It's a new scheme of Jeffrey's. We could make money by making freshly-made sandwiches to order and delivering them to airliners as they pass overhead.'

'...and anyway...' mumbled Jeffrey.

'What?'

'She's a girl.'

Dark indignation swept over Colette's face, as if she were a Trump mistaken for an Obama. Her voice could have cracked windows (if not skulls): 'So, I suppose that, in your view, being 'a girl' means I know nothing about managing the fluctuating core temperature so as to ensure that fatigue stresses on reactor coolant pipes don't lead to premature cracking?'

There was a pause which, if it could have been bottled, would have made an excellent paint stripper.

Jeffrey stood frozen while his brain recovered from what was, evidently, a major, *major,* miscalculation. After his brain reset, his opinion of his cousin had been completely revisited, reviewed, revoked and revised.

Besides, she had this cute little flower pinned to her dress...

<Author: What is it about decapitated flowers that seem so appealing? Ones that are, in fact, slowly dying of dehydration. Gasping their final gasps as it

were, before one's very own eyes. And yet this pathetic visage of a slowly dying flower seems romantic to us. Mind you, think about what flies find attractive. But I digress...>

He beckoned to her. 'It's this way.'

She rose from her chair and followed him out the door, the atmosphere visibly cooling as they left. From the corridor Humphrey heard her ask: 'How do you manage the recoil from the bungee cords? I've even tried using multiple Velcro stacks, but...' and her voice faded into the distance.

'Well...' said Bernadette after they'd gone. 'Shall I be Mother?'

'Oh. Do you think that's wise? After all we're closely related and the children...'

'No, you daft bear! Shall I pour the tea?'

'Oh. Oh! Oh, yes. Sorry. Sorry! Oh dear... I didn't mean...'

'The reason I came, apart from being sociable, is to discuss Aunt Bessie's departure and her legacy.'

'Where is she going? What's wrong with her leg...?' Humphrey knew immediately that he'd misheard and/or misunderstood Bernadette by the exasperated look on her face.

'She died Humphrey. She's dead. She has since ceased to share, care or swear. She whoofs her custard no more. She no longer drinks spirits, but in fact has become one. I'm here to talk about her estate.'

'Was it her leg that killed her?'

'Pardon? What on earth are you wittering about?'

'Ah! Sorry. When you said '...Aunt Bessie's departure and her leg you see...' I thought...' His voice tailed off. Humphrey thought furiously. She didn't have any land and didn't own an estate car as far as he could recall. Besides, how could a gammy leg kill someone? Unless someone had pulled it off and hit her over the head with it.

Bernadette huffed impatiently. Then: 'Her *estate,* Humphrey. What remains in her Will!'

'Oh! Yes. Sorry.'

So, perhaps he was wrong. Perhaps she did own land, or a car and have a bad leg. And who was Will? Her new toy boy? He didn't want to sound too stupid so he thought he'd listen on. Besides, she looked irritated and Humphrey was not a brave bear.

'As you know, Bessie was very keen on painting. She painted a lot. An awful lot. A lot of awful paintings in fact. She left explicit instructions that these paintings were to be kept as family heirlooms and preserved for future generations such that they may be enjoyed in the decades to come. It was her last wish that they must be displayed in a gallery for all eternity.'

'I seem to remember her painting goats in Sou'westers and wellington boots. Is that what you mean?'

'Yes. Goats in raincoats, Sou'westers, anoraks, t-shirts, skiing outfits, pink frilly tutus, short sexy kilts, nylon stockings, sheer mankinis and goodness knows what else. All in the worst possible taste, and none of them in perspective either.'

'Oh dear. How many of them are there?'

'Dozens,' she replied flatly. 'I promise you, the image of a goat wearing a floral baby-doll nighty and looking seductively over her shoulder will haunt you for the rest of your life.' She shuddered.

'Oh dear.'

'Yes. 'Oh dear' indeed. We need somewhere to display them indefinitely, preferably in an underground sealed vault. And it was noted that your gang lives in an extensive underground maze of tunnels and rooms. Perhaps you could house them for us?'

Humphrey pondered the task.

'What's in it for me?'

She sipped calmly at her tea. 'Twenty packets of various chocolate biscuits, including at least one, maybe more, of your favourites. What do you say?'

'Deal!'

'Wonderful! I shall let the others know. Now then, there's one other item that I need to resolve before you give me your usual boring tour of your home, chat about not-dogs who live in trees and Godalming's local river monster.'

Humphrey nodded, not paying attention. In his mind he was trying to sort out what needed to be moved in the kitchen cupboards to make room for this wonderful new treasure.

'She left you a small inheritance too.'

'She did?' Humphrey's ears perked up and stiffened in expectation.

'Yes. But you've already agreed to accepting those twenty packets of various chocolate biscuits, including at least one, maybe more, of your favourites. Haven't you?'

'Uhm, yes?'

'Good. It's settled then. We are in agreement. Now tell me about Godfrey, Jeffrey and those pesky squirrel-like scribbles. What have they been up to?' She sipped her tea.

Something in Humphrey's brain felt that something was amiss. It was as if he'd been given a puzzle but one of the pieces didn't fit.

On the other hand, twenty packets of biscuits. Chocolate biscuits no less. He was rich!

...but was that payment or was that inheritance?

Who cares! Twenty packets of chocolate biscuits! Yay!

*****

Should you ever come to Godalming and manage to take a tour of Humphrey, Jeffrey and

Godfrey's home, you will find, to your surprise, that deep underground there is a small art gallery. One that the Furricious Gang never visit, well at least on purpose, and would prefer not to visit at all. However, even more surprisingly, every now and then a delegation of reverential scribbles come from far and wide to pay a small fee (in chocolate biscuits of course) and admire these secret, sobering, and sometimes 'provocative' works of 'capricious' art.

Godalming Events

Regency 1811 – 1837
1836 – Godalming Police Force established.
1818 – Last public hanging in Godalming, on the Lammas Lands.
1813 – Wey Navigation extension to Arun above Pulborough started.

THE MEAL

by Ian Honeysett

'Are you sure this is the right place, Dad?' asked my daughter, Rachel.

'How do you mean? It's the restaurant for this hotel, isn't it?'

'Hotel? It's more like a fairy-tale castle! No, what I mean is that it's, well, so different to where we normally stay. You know, house-swaps. Where we have to persuade people to swap Rostok or Limerick for Godalming. Where we end up staying in a house remarkably similar to our own. But this is… well… look at it. It's just… huge and so… well, impressive. It just doesn't look like the sort of place we would ever stay or eat at. Just saying.'

I looked around. We were standing outside a very swish restaurant in the grounds of a French chateau that we had somehow booked on a special offer. The chateau was now a grand hotel but in the off-season. Its massive white walls – with just a hint of mildew- towered above us. And as you strained your neck looking up, pointed blue-grey roofs with what resembled tiny bell-towers on top. Huge chimneys, as tall as a house. And the long, narrow windows – French windows in fact. We felt quite tiny in comparison.

'It's been a long day,' commented my wife, Elizabeth, quite accurately. 'So let's enjoy ourselves this evening. Tomorrow we can slum it.'

The delicious smells of French cuisine beckoned us in. A heady mixture of boeuf bourguignon, Soupe à l'Oignon Gratinée, Quiche au Saumon et Crevettes and perhaps a little Mousse au Chocolat. Or was that my imagination? Anyway, we were famished. I reached out to open the ornate front door. It looked like an off-cut from the Palais de Versailles. All gold and fleury. It was also quite heavy and Rachel had to help me as I gripped the solid metal handle. Ouch! Had I cut myself? Instinctively I licked my hand and tasted the sticky splash of blood. A metallic appetiser perhaps?

Suddenly there was a tsunami of bright light from within. The Maitre-d, I assumed, not having met that many, had no doubt spotted us and opened the door. He had a large round and very pink face. Slicked-down black hair. Dyed? And an enormous smile with his perfect white teeth –apart from one crooked front tooth which, once seen, I couldn't ignore. I was about to speak when he oozed: 'Bonsoir, monsieur, Mesdames. Welcome.' Somehow he had guessed we were English. Most disappointing as I was keen to try my 'O' level French for the first time in over 20 years. Peut-etre I'd not forgotten quite all of it?

*****

He quickly led us to a table in the far corner. Why that one I wasn't sure as the restaurant was completely empty – apart from us. Every sound echoed.

'Dad, it's huge inside too!' gasped Rachel. 'It's like a museum with smells!'

Indeed it was. I looked around. Starched white table-cloths. Glinting sets of cutlery – surely a drawer-full on each table. Sparkling crystal glasses. Flowers on every table. The waft of their delicate scent tantalised my nostrils. Chairs with amazingly high backs made of gold and plush red velvet. You could almost taste the opulence. A thought quickly popped into my mind: the holiday might have been fairly cheap but this meal was most certainly not going to be. But, hey, it was too late to turn back though my bank account was telling me to do just that.

We sat down. The chairs were rather hard. No sinking down into them. None of that feeling when you just relax into the upholstery. Another waiter suddenly appeared and unfolded our enormous swan-like serviettes and gently spread them across our laps. We were immediately presented with huge menus and a hefty wine menu. It resembled a posh telephone directory.

I had that taste in my mouth that told me that there was going to be nothing on these menus that would be a pleasant surprise in terms of price. Before plunging in, I looked around again and could see that there were four waiters looking at us with keen anticipation. I desperately wanted some other diners to join us. An evening with so many eyes fixed on us made me feel quite squeamish. I became aware of chamber music playing gently in the background. Someone had turned the machine on. 'Tiddle, diddle, om pom... tiddle diddle om pom...' I almost expected to see a string quartet appear in the corner in their powdered wigs and knee breeches. Perfect. Probably Mozart though I doubted he could have afforded to eat here. The elaborate gilt and mirrored décor looked as though it dated from his time too.

'So what are you going to have, Dad?' Rachel's voice echoed in the sheer emptiness of the salon.

'Is there a set meal?' I asked rather forlornly. In my heart I already knew the answer.

'Not that I can see,' replied Elizabeth. 'But they do have an awful lot of sea-food. I just love sea-food. You can almost smell the prawns and crab. I wonder if they have lobster? It's years since we've had lobster.'

There was a good reason for that, I thought to myself as I began to peruse the menu. The pages were stiff like vellum. Each dish was described in mouth-watering detail. And there were so many of them. I dare not look at the prices as I had no desire to lose my appetite.

One of the waiting waiters began to walk towards us. His every step clicked on the parquet flooring. I almost expected him to salute.

'Are you ready to order some wine, monsieur? Perhaps I might recommend the...'

He mentioned something that included a date and a chateau but I replied: 'I just need a little time to read this excellent list, please.' He smiled at that. Clearly I knew what I was doing. Hardly likely to choose the second cheapest wine, eh?

'This wine looks nice, dear. A 2006 Château Puysserguier. It says that it's a white Saint Chinian from Languedoc. Soft and buttery with a hint of acacia flower, honey and spice.'

I looked for the price and was pleasantly surprised.

'Looks fine to me,' I said.

'An excellent choice, madam, monsieur,' commented the waiter with a hint of disappointment in his voice that it wasn't a premier cru – or whatever it's called.

*****

Ordering the food took some time as we all changed our minds several times to something more expensive each time. Apart from me of course.

The rest of the meal passed in a haze. Everything tasted as rich and satisfying as it smelt. From the subtle Mediterranean seafood salad, the succulent, melt-in-the mouth beef to the crispy, creamy, not quite burnty delight of the crème brulee. The salon was replete with a glorious Boullabaise of spicy, crabby, garlicky, meaty, fruity aromas. My nostrils almost collapsed with the onslaught. The visual highlight was when 3 waiters each with a silver domed cloche marched gingerly towards our table, took up position behind each of us and, at a secret sign, dramatically removed the cover with synchronised panache. We almost applauded.

When we finally finished eating, I noticed the others looking expectantly towards me.

'Delicious!' I exclaimed. They both nodded.

'Easily the best meal I've ever tasted,' beamed Rachel.

I requested l'addition in a revealingly tremulous tone. It was produced with a flourish. Eventually I dared to read it. My internal organs began to dissolve.

'Are you well, monsieur?' enquired the waiter. Had my face betrayed my despair?

'Sorry?' I replied.

'It's just that you appear to be bleeding.'

I looked at my hand and, sure enough, it was scarlet. And throbbing. I had quite forgotten about it with the excitement of the evening.

'Oh, yes, I cut myself on the door handle as we were coming in. I didn't realise it was bleeding quite so much.'

'That is most unfortunate, monsieur. Most unfortunate. Please excuse me for one moment.'

'Hey Dad,' whispered Rachel, 'do you think they'll take some money off for your injury?'

'Perhaps they'll waive the bill entirely?' suggested Elizabeth. 'I've heard of that happening.'

The mere thought suddenly made the chair so much comfier.

The waiter returned. Clicking his way across the floor. I felt all butterflies within. Was he about to make my day?

'I am so sorry for your injury, monsieur,' he gushed. 'So I have brought you a plaster. Now, will you be paying by credit card?'

Godalming Events

Edwardian 1901 -1914
1912 – Jack Phillips died – Titanic's telegraphist.
1911 – Last Court Baron held at the King's Arms and Royal Hotel.
1907 – Town Council moved from Pepperpot to New Council Offices in Bridge Street.

KATE'S STORY: A SEQUEL TO 'WHY DID HE DO IT?' IN GODALMING TALES 2

by Christine Butler

Kate had made the right choice when she married James Arnold in 1891. They enjoyed over 50 years together and had two daughters, Violet and Mabel. Her daughters first heard about their previously unknown Bennett relatives at her funeral in May 1945. She had been ill for nearly a year and Violet had eventually moved back home to Bournemouth to look after her. Their father James had not coped well with Kate's illness. He suffered from stress and ended up in hospital with a broken hip after a fall. He was still there when she died in the same hospital and he missed the funeral, much to his sorrow.

To some extent the two sisters were relieved that he was not there, as he might have been upset about their conversation with mysterious Cousin John. After the service he had approached them and introduced himself as John Wilson, a nephew of the deceased. 'I saw the notice of Kate Arnold's death in the local paper and I was hoping to meet her son Walter. Is he here? I knew Walter when I was a child and recently I've been trying to find him,' he explained.

The sisters were stunned by this. 'Kate Arnold didn't have a son. You're mistaken,' Vi replied, taken aback.

'Yes, she did, when she was Kate Bennett. He lived with us for a while in Woking but our families lost touch when I married and moved away. He had a brother Edward but I don't remember ever meeting him. My mother told me to treat Walter as my big brother because Edward was a long way away in Dorset and Walter missed him.'

'But we'd have known about them, surely. I know Mother was a widow when she married Father in 1891 but there weren't any children, I'm sure of that. You must mean a different Kate. Bennett's a common enough name.' Mabel was upset at the thought of their mother keeping a secret like that from them all their lives and cross with John for implying it.

'The two boys were looked after by Kate's mother Jane Wilson, when they were young.' John tried to convince the sisters. 'She was my grandmother too, but I had a different grandfather 'cause she married twice.'

'No, I'm sorry. That doesn't help because we never met either of our grandmothers.' Vi and Mabel walked away, unwilling to continue the conversation.

Paste sandwiches, cheese and crackers and home-made cakes awaited the mourners at their parents' house. On the way back there from the church Vi said, 'Well, we know there's no mention of Edward or Walter in Mother's will, just us and Father. Though their existence could account for why she bothered to make a will when she had so little to leave us.'

'I know Grandma had brothers and sisters and that she married twice so I suppose he could be distantly related to us. Thinking about it, Wilson could have been Grandma's surname.'

A few days later the sisters were busy preparing their parents' home for their father's return from hospital. A neighbour had helped them bring one of the two single beds down from their old room so that he could sleep downstairs in the parlour. The gate leg table was folded against the wall and one of the arm chairs had been moved to the back kitchen.

Vi planned to stay and look after him, having no home of her own now and no husband. Their Portsmouth house had received a direct hit in a South Coast air raid in 1944. Her husband had been at home nursing an injury received while on a Home Guard exercise the previous week and he had been killed.

The WRVS had been so kind to Vi when she was bombed out. She had been busy working for them in another part of the city when it happened. Now tidying away their mother's things she and Mabel sorted Kate's newer clothes into carrier bags ready to donate to them.

'Most of these clothes are too old-fashioned to pass on,' commented Vi, carefully re-folding a long, panelled skirt. 'But I might be able to alter this when I have time, and wear it myself.'

'Hm, Mother was much slimmer than either of us. We obviously take after Father,' Mabel replied thoughtfully, lifting out the contents of a drawer while her sister turned her attention to the top shelf of the wardrobe.

They had been hoping to find letters or documents that might throw some light on what Cousin John had told them. Was it really true that they had two half-brothers, brought up by their grandmother Jane Wilson? If so why hadn't they been told about them before? The sisters had never met Grandma Wilson and their mother rarely mentioned her or their step-grandfather. There must have been a family row years ago. Did they now have a clue about the cause?

'Mabel, I think I've found something. There's a leather suitcase on top of the wardrobe. Can you take it from me if I lift it down?' Vi passed the case to her sister and climbed down from the kitchen chair she had been standing on.

Mabel tried to open the case on the bed, then said, 'I saw a key that might fit this lock. It's in Mother's jewel box on the dressing table.' She looked in the almost empty box and found the key, trying it eagerly in the rusty lock. After a bit of persuasion it worked and she opened the case.

'What's in it? Are there any letters?' asked Vi, peering in. Half a dozen small cardboard boxes were packed neatly inside. Mabel lifted one out to show her.

'I think there might be,' she replied, putting the box back and closing the case. 'Let's take these downstairs and look through them carefully before we do anymore searching here. I know we're supposed to be turning stuff out but we've made an awful mess.'

'Come on then. I'll make us some tea. I think we'll need it handling dusty old papers.'

*****

Fifteen minutes later they were settled at the kitchen table drinking tea with the boxes from the case spread out between them. Vi selected a box and opened it carefully. 'Look, here's an old Valentine's card and a wedding photo. Is that Father?'

'Yes, I think so.' Mabel peered over Vi's shoulder. 'Is there anything written on the back?'

'30th September 1891 – such a happy day, in Mother's writing. It doesn't seem right going through drawers and the wardrobe in their bedroom with Father still in hospital,' Vi said thoughtfully.

'I think we must do it now, in case he just throws most of Mother's things out without going through them first. People do, you know.'

'That might be for the best, in the circumstances. Suppose he doesn't know about Mother's other children, assuming what John told us is true? This way we can make sure he doesn't find out about them from her old papers.'

208

They went on searching through the contents of the boxes, finding treasures such as birthday cards they had given Kate, envelopes containing letters from them, a few photographs, bills and a small note book used for household accounts. Picking up the last box Vi lifted the lid and exclaimed, 'Guess what's in this shoebox.'

'Shoes by any chance?' asked Mabel.

'Old fashioned buttoned ones with a small heel. They're beautifully made in soft leather and hardly worn.' Vi lifted them out gently and handed one to her sister.

'I hope we don't have bad luck now, putting these on the table. Oh, look, there's a card underneath them.' She picked up the card and read, 'To darling Kate with my love, Edmund, October 1882. Wrong date for a birthday present.'

'I've seen these shoes before. I think Mother offered them to me when I was 18. I tried them on but they were too small for me.' Vi examined the shoes, turning them over to look at the soles. 'Too old fashioned as well but I didn't say that to Mother. She said they were a bit tight for her feet and that was why she had hardly worn them. I didn't see the card then, of course.'

'She didn't offer them to me,' said Mabel, slightly peeved.

'No, your feet are bigger than mine.'

'Only slightly. Let's put these boxes back in the case and examine that small package tied up with string. It's the last item left.' String and paper must be saved during war time so Mabel patiently untied the knots, releasing the crackly brown paper from around a small biscuit tin. There was a faded picture of a thatched cottage on it. She opened the tightly-fitting lid gingerly.

'What's in it, Mabel? What have you found?'

'Two more envelopes but these look older.' She took one out and peeped inside. Her eyes lit up as she said, 'I think this might help to solve the mystery. It's a marriage certificate.'

'But we've already found that downstairs with Mother's Will. We know she was married before because it says she was a widow.'

'Exactly,' said Mabel. 'This must be the earlier one.' Unfolding it with care she flattened it on the table and read, 'Edmund Bennett, bachelor aged 18 and Kate Sargeant, spinster aged 19, married on the 9th October 1882 in Pentridge, Wareham. So it looks as though John could be right. That was nine years before our parents married. Plenty of time for two sons to be born.'

'Yes, but why were we never told about them and why were they brought up by our grandmother? Can you remember when she died?'

'No, I can't. It was too long ago. Let's see what else is in the tin.' Mabel took out something wrapped in tissue paper and found a pair of baby's bootees knitted in blue wool. She held them up.

'Baby Edward's or Baby Walter's I wonder?' Vi exclaimed.

'Worn by both I expect. They look well-washed. There's an envelope underneath them. Perhaps it contains the birth certificates.' She picked it up and slipped out the paper inside. It was a letter. With the late afternoon sun shining through the kitchen window she opened the letter out on the table. A shaft of light illuminated it as though it was signalling the answer to their questions. 'Oh, Vi, listen to this,' she gasped, then began reading the letter aloud:

Dear Kate,

Your letter arrived like a bolt out of the blue. Yes, I visited Bournemouth for Seth's funeral and met up with my other brothers there. It did not occur to me that you might be back living in the area or that someone would give you my address.

Yes, I did miss the boys. But I told myself that they would be well cared for living with you and your mother and I tried not to worry about them. Life was difficult enough, finding work as an inexperienced boot maker and somewhere to live. Annie gave birth to our first child in 1886, about six months after we settled in a small house in West London. I worked as a boot repairer but that didn't last and we moved to Godalming in Surrey.

The only way I could cope with missing out on the boys' childhood and not knowing how they were getting on was to assume they had died. I feel awful about that now. Are they married with children of their own? Of course, you don't know that either, do you, from what you say in your letter? I find it heart-breaking and wish you had not told me.

No, Annie and I never married. As you say, it did not seem necessary. Sometimes I regretted leaving you and the boys in the lurch, but when Annie, or Phoebe as she was still known, found she was expecting a baby, she gave me a difficult choice. Then it became impossible to marry after Ethel was born as people would know she was illegitimate. Anyway, it would have made me a bigamist for all I knew.

I know I was a cad. As you say, you and I were too young when we married but I know that is no excuse.

I am not decided yet whether I will send you this letter. I was surprised and shocked to receive yours, but pleased too in a way. We had some happy times together, didn't we?

Yours sincerely,

Edmund.

'Well, now we know for sure,' said Vi, looking thoughtful. 'And what it makes us.'

THE HAMMER

by Julie Buckingham

It must have been back in 1966 that dad brought the hammer home, and he showed it to us the next evening. It was a vicious-looking claw-hammer with a knobbly large head about the width of a fifty-pence piece supported by a long, thick handle. It looked dangerous – and heavy.

I held it in my little girl's hand, in fascination, for about a second, then gave it back to him, with a grimace, 'Ugh! It's all sticky on the handle!'

'Is it? Let's have a look!' Dad turned the hammer's handle over. 'Christ! You're right! Look here, Rene – ' he appealed to my mum. 'There's blood on it!'

'Are you sure it's not paint?' asked my mum, peering short-sightedly at the handle.

'It's blood, Rene! Blood doesn't smell like paint!' Mum and Dad stared at the handle in horror.

It was clear someone had had an accident with that hammer, or they might have been murdered with it! A frisson of excitement swept through me, and I found myself imagining all sorts of horrors.

Dad was saying: 'It was dark, and I saw this bloody thing lying in the gutter on my way to take out the last bus from the depot. Something must have happened there, Rene!'

My mum's green eyes widened. 'Do you suppose someone's been done in with it?'

'Hope not, this could be a murder weapon for all I know...'

'Oh, Ken, why did you pick it up?'

'Because I wanted it. I thought it had fallen out of some labourer's bag – honest! I didn't know it was covered in blood!'

'What are you going to do with it?' asked Mum.

'I don't know... Sit tight and hold onto it, I suppose... We'll see if there's any news on the radio about any 'activities' happening in our area!'

'The telly news will be on soon!'

'Hmm, I doubt it will mention anything for Guildford – not unless it's very bad!'

'Oh, Ken, trust you to pick it up! If it's a murder weapon you'll be an accessory, and by bringing it here, you've probably rubbed off the murderer's prints!'

'Let's not jump to conclusions, dear... We'll see what the news has to offer!'

'But what will you do if it turns out to be a murder weapon?'

'I'll wash it and keep it as if nothing has happened!' was my dad's cool reply. He bent down to me, who was all eyes and ears. 'You don't know anything about this, June, okay?'

'But, Daddy, you mustn't tell lies. Mummy says it's bad to fib! The bogey-man will come after you!'

'It's okay,' Dad soothed me, 'this will sort itself out, so don't you worry, pet!'

But he did worry. So did Mum. The pair of them watched the evening news avidly, sitting straight and expectant like a pair of soldiers on sentry duty. Mum relaxed a little, when the news was over.

'Nothing on there,' she said. 'Bed, now, June – say goodnight to Dad!'

So I went to bed dreaming that a man was chasing me in the dark, a dirty great hammer in his hand.

*****

We often visited my aunt and uncle, who lived in Farncombe, and we used to gather at The White Hart pub on a Saturday evening. Kids were not allowed inside in those days, but as the landlord knew us well, he let me come in. I remember my dad went to the bar to order a second round of drinks. Men were drinking around the bar, deep in conversation, and the whole pub was full of people talking and glasses tinkling. I followed Dad because I wanted a packet of Smith's crisps, which fascinated me; I used to imagine the little blue salt bag inside was buried treasure!

A man my dad knew engaged him in conversation which I overheard: 'Hi, Ken! Shame about Dick West, isn't it?'

'Dick West, the odd-job man? Why – what's happened to him?' asked my dad.

'He's dead! Died last Saturday night, outside the bus depot – poor sod!'

'But he could only have been thirty-something – too young to die!'

'He was murdered – Police think with a mallet of some kind!'

'Good God! How awful! How do you know this, Reg?'

'It was on the early morning radio news yesterday. Police are still hunting for the murder weapon, it's claimed.'

'Oh, God!' Dad groaned. He looked down at me. 'Angel, go back to Auntie's table, please – I'll bring your crisps over!'

'But, Dad – !'

'Off you go, now, please, June!' Dad flapped his hands at me grimly. He looked pale and sick. I heard him mutter to Reg: 'Who did this terrible murder, I wonder? Poor Dick!'

'Don't know. Apparently, Dick was loaded with cash. It was probably a gang of hooligans after his money! Here, do you want another pint?'

'No thanks, Reg. All of a sudden I don't fancy any more to drink!'

*****

I was bundled off to bed earlier that night, whilst Mum and Dad had a 'talk'. But, being me, I crept down our steep stairs in our two-up, two-down semi, and listened at the backroom door to what they were saying.

I heard Dad speaking worriedly: 'This is awful! I don't know what to do, Rene.'

'Well, you can't destroy the evidence by washing the hammer now,' Mum said.

'Christ! I wish I'd never picked up the blooming thing! The trouble it's caused me!'

'And me! You men – you must pick up things out of curiosity! Now look at the worry it's caused! Never, ever, do this thing again, Ken!' She was really angry with him, for my mum was usually a placid woman. Tonight, she was a raging bull, a startled out-of-her-depth female, protecting her boundaries.

'I'm sorry, pet. I'll never do it again!'

'I can't have the police coming round here to arrest you on suspicion of murder! They'll think you did it! Whatever will I tell the neighbours? Old Ma Atkins next door is a nosy devil and she'll tell everyone in the street!'

'But it was instinct – !'

217

'Instinct be dammed!' Mum was still ranting. 'I'll not have any trouble be brought to this house! Pick up things off the street if you must, but not bloody hammers!'

Then the doorbell rang –

'Who could that be at this time of night?' wondered dad.

Mum said, sourly: 'The police, probably!'

I wondered, too, but quickly slipped upstairs, to stand, listening from my bedroom door. I heard the door-latch being unlocked, and strained my ears, fearful that Dad was going to be arrested.

'Evening, sir. Sorry to call on you at this late hour, but needs must.'

My dad stared at the looming policeman standing grimly in front of him – he must have been startled to death! 'Oh! Er, w-what can I do for you officer? If this is anything to do with Dick West – I know nothing about it!'

There was a blank pause.

'Who is Dick West?' asked the constable.

'The poor man who was murdered in Guildford, outside the bus depot!' my dad blurted out.

'Oh, *that* murder! Huh! It's been proved that it's not a murder; the bloke you're talking of slipped on the pavement, and gashed his head so badly, that he died from it!'

'But I hear hooligans stole all his money and that he was hit on the head with a mallet!'

'That's right; they were opportunists, they made off with a few bob but we got them now, under lock and key! We found no mallet.'

'Then, why did you knock on my door?'

'Oh, yes... Well I assume that Hillman Minx parked outside here is yours?' Dad nodded dumbly. 'It's only to tell you that someone's cracked your car's offside light. Afraid there's been a spate of car smashing lately! Just thought I'd let you know!'

'Good God! Then you're not going to arrest me?'

'Why should I do that, sir? You've not committed any offence!'

Dazed, Dad muttered something about withholding evidence, but luckily, the policeman didn't hear him. I held my breath, thinking: '*Please Daddy, don't say anymore*!'

Sorry about your car, but it's the only one in the street. You'll get it mended soon I should think! Goodnight, sir, I'll be on my way!'

Relief spread through Dad's worried face. Slumping beside the door frame, he said, weakly. 'Goodnight, officer... er... thanks.'

He watched, as the man in uniform, who had inadvertently given him such tremendous good news, walked smartly away.

As to THAT hammer, it was kept in Dad's shed for years and years and years – and no doubt used from time to time (although Mum never allowed it into the house)! Whether it had been a murder weapon or not, none of us ever found out!

Godalming Events

Georgian 1714 – 1811
1782 – Town Bridge over Wey built replacing the Bishop's Bridge.
1764 – Wey Navigation extended from Guildford to Godalming.
Godalming Wharf opened.
1761 – French prisoners from Belle Isle Expedition in the Seven Years' War held in the Market Hall.
1726 – Mary Tofts claimed that she had given birth to 18 rabbits.

A SECOND CHANCE

by Pauline North

Ginny settled herself in her chair, pleased to have claimed her favourite table in the Waitrose café. She considered this in itself a stroke of luck as most of the tables were taken, the café, as usual, was crowded.

Once a week, usually on Thursday, Ginny caught the bus from Farncombe into Godalming to do her main shop of the week. This had been, for far too long, the highlight of her week. She would always dress with care and always, after the shopping was done, drop in to the café for a coffee and a cake. Where, surrounded by chatter and laughter, she could almost feel included.

Usually she would have a paper or a book with her, so she could appear occupied. Not on this day. This was her birthday and she wanted to take in every moment. Hear the chatter. See the bright sunshine making patterns on the tables, the smiling faces. Ginny had decided that her 65th birthday would be a happy day, her son had sent a card and she had a new pair of shoes, prettily gift wrapped, waiting at home to be opened, her gift to herself.

*****

The man in the far corner had been studying the other customers, or at least the women, the ones

sitting alone. There were only two. One was working on a laptop, her long dark hair scrunched into an untidy ponytail. His eyes moved on.

There, at a table on the side wall, a much more likely candidate. Sixty something he guessed, about the same age as himself, well presented with carefully styled hair. He noticed a couple of good diamond rings on manicured hands.

He sat up straight and looked for an opportunity to make contact. The chance came when a mother with two small children walked past the woman. The younger child, desperate to walk beside his mum, knocked the woman's arm as she took a sip of her coffee. The mother grabbed the child, told him off loudly and dragged him away. The woman mopped the slopped coffee with her napkin then looked quickly around, a little embarrassed; to see how many people realised that there had been an incident.

He managed to catch her eye and smiled sympathetically. Perhaps this new town, Godalming, would prove to be a worthwhile move after all.

*****

When Ginny stood to leave, gathering up her shopping bags she noticed the man at the corner table, the rather handsome one who had smiled at her, was also preparing to leave.

Outside the store she paused to breathe in the soft summer air and raise her face to the sun before walking to the roadside, where she waited to cross the road to the bus stop. One of her bags was particularly heavy; she had treated herself to quite a few treats. As she stood waiting for a break in the traffic one of the handles gave way and spilled shopping onto the pavement.

While she scrabbled to pick up her shopping, crouching rather unsteadily on the pavement, the man from the café appeared beside her and helped retrieve the last few items. Somehow between them they managed to stuff everything into the other two bags.

'Thank you, that was very kind,'

'Not at all, a pleasure to help.'

'I had better get these over to the bus stop.'

They both looked down anxiously at the bulging bags.

'Impossible those bags are too heavy to carry by the handles, they need lifting from underneath, there's no way you can manage those on the bus. Look, my car is in the car park, let me give you a lift home.'

'Well, yes, that would be most helpful, thank you.'

The first bag was lifted and carefully placed in her arms.

'My name is Tommy.' he said.

'Ginny.'

On the way to Farncombe, following Ginny's directions, Tommy congratulated himself on his stroke of luck. Fancy the bag breaking like that; he couldn't have managed anything better if he had planned it himself. Even better, when they reached Ginny's house and he had helped her carry the shopping indoors, she offered him a cup of tea.

Driving back to his small flat above a shop in Godalming high street, Tommy reviewed his progress, although the house had been smaller, much smaller than he had hoped that didn't mean there wasn't a nice nest egg tucked away. The plus side was that the woman, Ginny, was really very nice so why not invest some time in her. He had arranged to take her to the cinema the next week. He began to sing quietly to himself.

The cinema visit was a success, they both enjoyed the film then afterwards Tommy took Ginny for a drink in the King's Arms. By the time she was on her second gin and tonic Ginny was nicely relaxed. Tommy managed to get her talking by asking if she had always lived in Godalming. By the end of the evening he knew most of her life story, that her husband had died some fifteen years before and that there was a son, living in Yorkshire, who rarely contacted her.

Speaking about the son had caused Ginny's voice to choke and she turned her head away. Tommy took the opportunity to show a little compassion by resting a hand on Ginny's where it rested on the table. After a few seconds she removed her hand and smiled brightly. 'There's quite a lot of interesting local history, for example, Peter the Great of Russia, once stayed right here at the King's Arms.'

At the end of the evening, when Tommy dropped Ginny at her home she rather nervously invited him in for a coffee. Tommy put on one of his best performances. His expression, at first showing enthusiasm, changed to noble self-control.

'That would be – I would like that, another time.'

He smiled, his best warm, yearning smile into her eyes, then leaned across to open her door, allowing just a little contact shoulder to shoulder.

Over the next few weeks they saw a lot of each other, they visited the theatre, spent days at the coast and long hours walking in the country. They laughed together at the same silly things, sang along together to music in the car. As Tommy slowly introduced a physical element to their relationship, he was delighted by how responsive Ginny proved to be.

On a gloriously golden late summer day Tommy took Ginny for a walk on Blackdown, a place she knew well. They wandered the sandy paths, breathed deep of the pine scented air. When they reached the white stone seat that looked out over a spectacular view Tommy sat and gestured for Ginny to join him.

She chatted on for a moment, pointing out the direction of villages and landmarks, then realising that Tommy was sitting very still and wasn't listening to her she sat and waited for him to speak. He took her hand and drew a deep breath.

'Ginny, you must know how much these last weeks have meant to me, I have never been so happy. I love you, very much, more than I believed possible and I like to think that maybe you love me a little too. Will you marry me?'

He took her in his arms and wiped away the tears that streamed down her face. From somewhere in the area of his chest he heard a muffled, 'Yes.'

That evening they celebrated with a meal at their favourite restaurant and toasted the future with champagne.

The wedding took place on a mild cloudy day in October, a simple service at the local register office with only a few people, Ginny's friends, to share their special day.

*****

Twenty years had passed; the crowd, outside the crematorium had been touchingly genuine with their condolences. Most of their many friends had been able to attend. The service, they all assured him, had been perfect and the music, chosen from Ginny's favourites, had been beautiful.

Slowly the mourners dispersed, to meet again at the hotel where food and drink were laid on. Tommy, barely aware of his surroundings moved from person to person, the men shook his hand, the women hugged him and then they left.

Tommy thanked the caterers then he went home. He drove through the cold October rain to the small house in Farncombe, to a home that was full of Ginny.

For twenty years they had been happy, more than happy, they had found joy in each day, in being together. Tommy had come to Godalming looking for a victim but to his eternal surprise he had found love. His proposal all those years ago had been genuine, every one of his words spoken from a transformed heart.

Godalming Events

Anglo-Saxon to 1066
c940 – Saxon defence point moved from Eashing burgh to Guildford.
c885 – Defensive Saxon burgh built at Eashing.
c820 - Anglo- Saxon carved stones in St Peter and St Paul (Godalming Parish Church)

I SAW YOU
by Alan Barker

Above him, the moon and stars shone brightly. Nothing stirred in Phillips Memorial Park; winter had already stripped the trees of their leaves and the local wildlife was sheltering from the cold.

Glyn shivered. The temperature must be close to freezing, he thought. But he'd had plenty of experience of extremes of weather, never more so than when serving in Afghanistan.

He checked his watch - one o'clock. Right on cue, he heard their voices in the distance, gradually getting louder.

The problem had been going on for two weeks. Every night he had been woken by these two loathsome girls: sauntering along the road singing at the tops of their voices, no doubt suitably merry after a night out in Godalming. And trying to get back to sleep had been beyond him.

Only recently he thought he had finally got over the insomnia that had plagued him since returning from Afghanistan 15 years earlier. He had been diagnosed with traumatic brain injury, having suffered a severe blow to the head from shrapnel. Rehab had helped - until now.

The night before last he had decided to stay up late and go out to speak to the girls, try and reason with them. But they had simply laughed and patted him on the cheek before continuing on their merry way towards the park.

Last night their singing had woken him yet again. He had lain there pounding his fist into the pillow, knowing it would be hours before he'd get back to sleep.

Now the girls were passing the bandstand, engrossed in their rendition of *Delilah*. From his overcoat Glyn pulled out his semi-automatic pistol - which he had stolen from an enemy corpse all those years ago - and screwed the silencer to the end of the barrel. It felt good, gave him a sense of control. Almost like being back in Kabul.

As the girls came closer he stepped out from behind the tree and blocked their path. The singing stopped abruptly.

'Something we can help you with, Big Boy?' the fair-haired girl said, smirking.

He said, 'The other night I asked you to cut out the singing. You keep waking me and then I can't get back to sleep.'

'So you thought you'd give us a little scare, did you? Ah, so sad!'

'It'll be sad for you if I have to use this,' Glyn said, raising the pistol. 'But very enjoyable for me.'

'Let's clear off, Donna,' the dark-haired girl said, tugging at her friend's arm. 'This guy's got a screw loose.'

'What's the problem? No saddo is going to scare me just because he's got a toy gun in his hand. Very enjoyable for me,' she mimicked him.

That was all Glyn needed. The pistol popped and Donna crumpled at his feet. The dark-haired girl followed a second later, a look of incredulity on her pretty face.

Within minutes he was back inside his flat, feeling distinctly heady.

*****

The following day, a Saturday, Glyn resolved to carry on as normal. But first there was something specific he needed to do. After a light breakfast he set off in his battered old Escort towards the rural village of Puttenham, his string bag tucked out of sight in the boot.

On reaching Cutmill Pond he walked for some way along the path then, satisfied there was nobody else in the vicinity, threw into the water the bag which contained his pistol and silencer and some heavy stones - it sank instantly. Taking his time, he retraced his steps and drove home.

In the car park he bumped into one of his neighbours, Mary Whittington, evidently on her way out somewhere. He said a polite 'hello' but got nothing in return, which was typical of her, he thought. She reminded him of Mrs White from the board game *Cluedo*.

Back in his flat he found an envelope on the doormat. Inside was a handwritten note, in block capitals:

I SAW YOU

Glyn gasped, staring at the message.

He could hardly believe someone had witnessed the shootings. He had felt sure he and the girls had been alone in the park.

Who had left the note? How long would it be before a second anonymous note arrived? Would he have to pay for silence?

A little later there was a knock on the door and Glyn thought it might be the blackmailer, come to discuss terms. But outside were a man and a woman - probably in their late twenties, he guessed - holding up badges. Glyn held his breath.

'Good morning, sir,' the man said. 'I'm Detective Constable Hardcastle and this is DC Jenkins. A serious incident took place last night in Phillips Memorial Park and we need to ask all local residents if they can help with our enquiries. May we come in for two minutes?'

He let the officers in and stayed by the door a moment. Now keep calm, he thought. Just say you slept all night and didn't hear a thing.

He walked back into the lounge - and froze.

The detectives had seated themselves and were looking at him expectantly. On the table between them was the anonymous note, where he had left it.

As calmly as he could he picked up the note and put it in the nearest drawer, as if tidying up. He prayed that neither detective had read it.

After what seemed an eternity DC Jenkins spoke. 'As my colleague mentioned, a serious incident took place last night. Two women were killed in the park and we wondered if you saw or heard anything?'

'Not a thing,' he replied, frowning.

DC Jenkins produced two photographs. 'These are the victims. Do you recognise either of them?'

One fair-haired girl and one dark-haired. He'd had mental images of them all night long. 'I can't say I do.'

'Were you here on your own yesterday evening?'

'Yes, I had a quiet night in.'

They got to their feet. 'Thank you for your time, sir. If you think of anything that may help please let us know.'

With mounting relief Glyn escorted the detectives to the front door. Just then the letter box squeaked open and something was pushed through, making him jump. Happily he recognised it as a communication from his phone provider.

Outside the postman was on his rounds. 'Buongiorno,' he said cheerfully.

Shuffling along the path towards them was old Mr Leadbetter from next door in flat one.

*****

The second anonymous note arrived that afternoon.

He yanked the door open. Heading towards her own flat, not in any obvious hurry, was Mary Whittington. He knew it was her the moment he saw the scruffy white cardigan.

Glyn shut the door and scrutinised the envelope, marked 'FLAT TWO'. He ripped it open and read the note: -

ONE GRAND IN CASH

LEAVE IN A BLACK BIN LINER UNDER BIG BLACK BIN IN COURTYARD BY 11 PM TOMORROW LATEST

OR ELSE

Glyn swore. Taking a deep breath, he made a coffee and considered his options.

Instinct told him not to pander to the blackmailer, otherwise further demands would no doubt follow. On the other hand he couldn't risk Mary spouting off to the police.

Should he silence her permanently? He no longer had his trusty pistol, but more importantly another murder would almost certainly make the flats the focal point for the killings of the two girls.

233

Glyn gazed out of the window. 'I SAW YOU,' the first note had read.

But what precisely *had* Mary seen? Surely it was stretching the imagination to think she had been in the park on such a bitterly cold night? And even if she had spotted him letting himself into his flat at gone one o'clock in the morning, how could she have known he had been responsible for the deaths of the two girls? The more Glyn mulled it over the less sense it made.

Presently he decided on a course of action.

*****

He knocked softly on the door of flat four. After a brief pause Mary Whittington appeared.

'Hello, Mary. Can I come in for a minute?'

She led him into her lounge and looked at him questioningly.

'You left me a note, Mary.'

'Yes?'

'I don't understand it.' He took a deep breath. 'I just want to know what you meant by the note.'

'It's nothing to do with me. I found it on my doormat when I got back from shopping. It said 'Flat Two' on the envelope, so I realised somebody put it through my door by mistake.'

Glyn thought quickly. Had the blackmailer delivered the note to Mary deliberately, thereby

234

trying to deflect Glyn's attention on to her as the possible blackmailer? Or was it just that the blackmailer didn't want Glyn to catch him - or her - popping the note through his letter box?

'So do you know who put the note through your door?' he asked.

'No, I was out at the time. I just told you.'

Glyn digested this information, then forced a smile. 'I'm sorry, Mary. There seems to have been a misunderstanding.'

He headed back to his flat, his mind in turmoil.

*****

Glyn spent the following day, Sunday, doing his weekly shopping and cleaning the flat.

He had destroyed the blackmailer's notes but memorised the details. He had been instructed to pay £1,000 in cash by eleven o'clock tonight. Well, he'd already decided he wasn't going to pay a penny.

He couldn't stop thinking about the blackmailer and speculating as to his or her identity. Hopefully he would find out later.

From his vantage point by the courtyard he kept a watchful eye over the bin area between eleven o'clock and half past midnight. No one came.

*****

Glyn went to work the following day.

When he arrived home he found a familiar envelope on his doormat. With a sinking feeling he picked it up and opened it.

I'M DISAPPOINTED

YOU NEED TO LEAVE ONE GRAND IN CASH IN A BLACK BIN LINER UNDER THE BLACK BIN BY TOMORROW (TUESDAY) 11 PM

THIS IS YOUR LAST CHANCE

Glyn screwed up the note and threw it across the room. Presently he poured himself a beer but only succeeded in crushing the plastic glass, the amber liquid spilling onto his lap.

*****

By Wednesday the weather had turned milder but misty. The man in the high-vis orange jacket sauntered along the path that encircled the flats, humming softly. Reaching the bin area, he dropped to his hands and knees and reached under the black bin, pulling out a black bin-liner. On opening it he gave a grunt of annoyance. Then a forearm clamped around his jaw, jerking his head backwards.

A voice whispered, 'Buongiorno, Mr Postman,' before something sliced along his neck and his body went slack.

*****

236

Glyn dropped the bloody knife into the black bin, then hauled the body behind the bin so that it wouldn't easily be seen. Blood was dripping down the green bin but there was nothing to be done about that. He looked up. Mr Leadbetter was staring at him, a bag of rubbish in his hand. Glyn stared back, open-mouthed. Three murders already. Now Mr Leadbetter stood in his way.

The thought of harming the old man appalled him.

Mr Leadbetter pointed a shaking finger. '*I saw you.*'

Galvanized, Glyn ducked past the old man and hurried back to his flat. Within minutes he had filled his rucksack and left, locking the door behind him. He didn't even glance at the old Escort as he strode past it, heading into the ever-thickening mist. A siren sounded in the distance and he thought of Mr Leadbetter dialling 999 with unsteady fingers.

Putting on his baseball cap, Glyn continued at a brisk pace along the main road towards Godalming station. Over the road a white Mercedes was edging out of a cul-de-sac, its right-hand indicator flashing orange. A police car emerged from the mist as the Mercedes accelerated sharply into the main road and swerved, mounting the pavement.

Glyn felt himself catapulted skywards and spinning in mid-air, before hitting concrete with a sickening jolt. He was vaguely aware of footsteps rushing up to him and a man saying:

'I'm so sorry, mate. I didn't see you.'

Godalming Events

Tudor 1485 – 1603
1601 – The Manor of Godalming sold by Queen
Elizabeth to Sir George Moore of Loseley.
1563 – Godalming constituted a market town by
statute.
1541 – The Manor of Godalming passed to the
Crown.

THE MURDER OF EMILY JOY: 1889

by Ian Honeysett

'Yes, my name is Mrs Joy. How can I help you?'

'I'm Adrian Hanozet, Mrs Joy, and I am a reporter with The Surrey Comet newspaper.'

'Are you indeed? It's not a paper I ever read, Mr Honeysett. So what is your business?'

'Mrs Joy, I have written a number of tales of murder in the Godalming area. Not sensational stories, you understand. Nothing like that. I have heard of the tragic events involving your dear daughter – late daughter – Emily a few years ago and wondered…'

'If I am sufficiently recovered to talk about it? I'm not sure…'

'I do understand of course. I can assure you mine would be a most sympathetic account, Mrs Joy. But, if it is still too soon…'

'No, please come in, Mr Honeycombe. In fact I think it might do me good to talk about it. After all, it was several years ago – back in 1889. So perhaps now is the time. Would you care for a cup of tea?'

'That would be most welcome, Mrs Joy.'

*****

239

'So, where to begin? Well, my dear Emily was just seventeen years old and living here in Church Street, Godalming with the rest of our family when she told me that she had met a young man named Ebeneezer Jenkins. She explained that he was seeking lodgings and wondered whether he might lodge with us? So I agreed that he should join us for dinner one evening and we would then decide whether he might take the small room above the kitchen. She stressed that he would pay rent of course. Times were hard – indeed still are – so that income would be very welcome.'

'And how did you find Ebencczer, Mrs Joy?'

'He seemed a pleasant young man. He was a couple of years older than Emily. He said that he came from a good family. He was due to inherit a large amount of money - £500 – when he reached 30 years of age. I asked him if he had a trade and he said that, in fact, he had a profession! He said he was an artist. I must admit my heart sank somewhat at that. But he quickly explained that he was a painter of theatrical scenery for touring companies. He said his work was much in demand and that he had an income of one pound a week! He said he confidently expected this to rise to two pounds a week in the near future.'

'Indeed. So what was your decision, Mrs Joy? Did you agree to take him in as a lodger?'

'We discussed the matter as a family once he had departed that evening. We all agreed we should offer him lodgings – though my other daughter,

Elizabeth, was not quite so enthusiastic it has to be said.'

'Why was that, Mrs Joy?'

'She wasn't sure but said that she thought there was something a little odd about him. But nothing she could put her finger on. She thought it rather strange when he asked us to call him 'Wheatcroft' – his professional name, he added. He said it was his mother's maiden name and he had always been very close to her. Anyway, we agreed to welcome him into the family. He joined us a few days later. Before long, Emily and Ebeneezer decided to become engaged. They planned to marry on 15th March. Everything seemed to be going so well.'

'So when did things change, Mrs Joy?'

'Emily told me that it seemed a little surprising that 'Wheatcroft' had never invited her to visit his studio. It was located in a rather secluded garden owned by a Mr Henderson not so far away but she had only glimpsed it from a distance. So she had never had an opportunity to see any of his artistic work. I told her to ask him direct if she might visit. The following evening – after supper – she raised the matter. He sought to change the subject – complimenting her on her beautiful brooch. She explained that inside it was a Queen Victoria Jubilee half-crown commemorating our dear Queen's Golden Jubilee the previous year. I feared she might allow herself to be diverted by this but she wasn't. He looked somewhat annoyed but had little option but to agree. He said he had to meet with an

241

acquaintance first at the Three Crowns Inn but that he would then be delighted to show her his studio and his latest commission. She looked so relieved.'

'Why was she relieved, Mrs Joy?'

'She had told me a couple of days before that she was beginning to suspect that he had not been entirely truthful with her about his background, his work as an artist or his income. She said she was beginning to have doubts about the wedding.'

'So were her fears allayed by her visit to the studio, Mrs Joy?'

'Not quite. That was the very last time we ever saw our dear Emily. The next occasion we saw 'Wheatcroft' was when he was in court charged with her murder.'

'A truly terrible experience for you all, Mrs Joy. Thank-you for sharing your story with me. I will now visit the landlord of the Punchbowl Inn in Hindhead for the next part of this tragic tale. Goodbye Mrs Joy. Thank-you so much.'

*****

'What would you like to drink, sir?'

'A pint of ale, please, landlord. My name is Adrian Hanozet and I am writing an account of the murder of Emily Joy back in 1889. I believe you, Mr Phillips, played a vital role in the matter?'

'I suppose I did, Mr Hanozet. As we're not so busy just now, I may have time to tell you about it. But let me pour your pint first.'

'Thank-you, Mr Phillips. Delicious! So please tell me how you became involved in this sorry business?'

'Indeed. Well, it's a day I will never forget, that's for sure. This very ordinary, rather slight individual, came into the Inn and ordered a pint. He didn't look well. I enquired whether he was alright? He replied that he had had something of a shock. I asked if there was anything I could do to help? We pride ourselves on our friendly service here at the 'Punchbowl Inn'.

'I'm sure you do. What did he say?'

'He spoke so quietly I could hardly make him out. He said that he thought he was quite beyond human help. I began to suspect he was going to tell me that he had no money to pay for the beer but, instead, he said that his fiancée, sweet Emily, had met with a cruel death. Naturally I asked him to explain. He replied that she had died the previous day. They had recently had some difficulties and had made a pact. What sort of pact, I enquired? A suicide pact, he said. I was rather taken aback by this as you can imagine. I wondered if he was making some kind of bizarre joke but he said he was being entirely serious. He drank half the pint and then said that they were due to be married but that she had begun to doubt whether he earned enough to support them both. I asked him what was his trade? He said that he painted theatrical scenery. Very successfully. Then his shoulders slumped and he admitted that, in fact, things had not been going too well. He had not had any commissions for some time and was heavily in debt.'

'So how did this lead to a suicide pact?'

'Exactly what I asked him, sir. He said that they both agreed that it would be better to die together than to be separated by financial circumstances. They decided to drown themselves in the River Wey. She threw herself in but he said he was too cowardly to do likewise and, not being a good swimmer, felt unable to save her. He simply watched her drown.'

'Were you convinced by his account, Mr Phillips?'

'No – his story seemed to lack all conviction. I asked if he had reported her death to the police? He said not. He asked if I disbelieved him? I replied that it seemed far more likely that she would cancel the wedding rather than decide to kill herself. He stared hard at me and then admitted that his story was pure fiction.'

'I see. So did he explain how exactly Emily did die? Assuming that any of his story was true.'

'Again, that is just what I asked him. I did wonder if he had already had too much to drink but he seemed perfectly sober. After a pause, when he seemed to go into a sort of trance, he explained that

Emily was indeed dead. And then he simply said: 'I killed her.''

'What did you say to that?'

'Well, I admit I have met all sorts of folk in my time as a Landlord but I had never heard anything like this! I just looked at him in case he was about to burst out laughing. But he looked quite serious. He said that he took her to his studio as she had asked him to and she saw immediately that it was virtually empty. She realised at once that all his claims to be a successful painter were entirely false. She asked if he had any money at all. He admitted that he had only debts. At this, she became very angry and began hitting him. He said he tried to calm her down but that, before he knew what he was doing, she was lying there on the floor. He supposed he must have hit her.'

'What did he do then?'

'This was one of the oddest things of all – he said that he simply locked up the studio and went straight to the Sun Inn in Godalming. He needed a drink. Speaking of which, your glass appears to be empty, sir. Would you like another?'

'An excellent idea, Landlord. And please have one yourself.'

'Don't mind if I do, sir. So, again, I asked if he had reported her death to the police? He said he hadn't. I told him that he must certainly do so and that I would take him myself to Guildford Police Station. He said he supposed I was right and that he

245

would come with me willingly. As soon as he had finished his pint of course.'

'And he did not attempt to escape?'

'Not at all – he was most co-operative, sir. When we arrived in Guildford, I asked him to tell the Police Sergeant exactly what he had told me and he did so. The Sergeant asked if he was confessing to murder? He replied that he supposed he was. The Sergeant then quickly informed Inspector Berry of his admission. The Inspector reminded him that the penalty for murder was death by hanging. Ebeneezer said that he fully deserved to hang. Inspector Berry then took a full statement from Mr Wheatcroft. He said he had no recollection of striking Emily but supposed he must have done so. He said he had immediately locked up his studio and gone to the Sun Inn for a drink. He had not been back home or to his studio since. Inspector Berry then arrested him for the murder of Emily Joy. He seemed almost relieved.'

'Thank-you, Mr Phillips, for your account. And for the excellent beer.'

'Where next, Mr Hanozet?'

'To speak with Deputy Chief Constable Barker of Surrey County Police. I believe he can advise me on the final stages of this tragic story.'

*****

'Many thanks for agreeing to see me, Deputy Chief Constable Barker. As you know, I am writing an account of the Emily Joy murder and understand that you are particularly familiar with the case?'

'Quite correct, Mr Hanozet. I was given Mr Wheatcroft or, to give him his actual name, Ebeneezer Jenkins', signed confession and a report of the constables who examined his studio in Mr Henderson's garden where they found the body of Miss Joy. They confirmed that her face was black, her nose was broken and a silk handkerchief was found stuffed in her mouth. The autopsy revealed that she had been outraged and then strangled with her own boa. When this was put to the accused, he replied that he was guilty and fully deserved to be hanged. When the case went to Court on 7th January 1889, he pleaded Guilty but Insane.'

'On what grounds did he claim insanity, sir? Was that the first time he made that claim?'

'I believe so. He said that he had been greatly affected by reading all the many accounts of the recent Whitechapel murders. By the way, the Inquest jury were so affected by the case that they declared that they wished to donate their fees to aid Mrs Joy with the funeral expenses of her dear daughter, Emily.'

'Was he found guilty but insane?'

'No, the jury rejected his claim. The Judge said that he had never known a crime committed under circumstances more shocking or revolting. He pronounced sentence: that Ebeneezer Jenkins be taken to a place of execution where he should hang by the neck 'til the body be dead. And the Lord have mercy upon his soul.'

'And did he have any final words before he was hanged?'

'He did. I have here an account by the Reverend Swallow, Chaplain at Wandsworth Prison. May I read it to you?'

'Please do so, Deputy Chief Constable.'

'It states that Ebeneezer Jenkins said to him these words: 'I am a spiritual person in my own way, Reverend. I was brought up by my dear mother, Mabel, who, thankfully, is still alive. It was a difficult life but I was determined to be successful. The problem was that I had few obvious abilities. Except for painting. I loved the theatre and wanted, more than anything, to be part of it. I tried acting but everyone told me that I was quite hopeless. Then I thought – perhaps I could paint theatre scenery? I painted some for a local theatre group in Milford and they liked it! So I borrowed some money and hired a studio. Then I met sweet Emily and my whole life changed. I wanted only to marry her so I assured her that I was a successful painter. The thing I feared more than anything in the world was that she would leave me if she knew that I had never actually been paid for my painting. When she discovered the truth that evening in my studio, I despaired. The details are so blurred but I assume she slapped me and that I then hit her. Although I am a slight fellow, I must have hit her very hard. She collapsed.' The Chaplain replied that Emily had been outraged before her death.

Ravished. Surely he would remember that? He said that he did not but that, since no one else was present there, he must have been guilty of the assault. He repented of his sins and said again that he deserved to hang.'

'I understand that the hanging itself was somewhat unusual?'

'Indeed. Ebeneezer Jenkins was a very slight fellow and so the executioner strapped 7 lb weights to his legs to ensure that the 6'6' drop would suffice. He was pleased to report that it was a great success.'

'You decided to attend Emily Joy's funeral in Godalming?'

'I did, as a mark of respect. Monday 14th January 1889. I recall it was a suitably overcast and gloomy day. There were between 3 and 4,000 mourners gathered at the cemetery. We had several police on hand in view of such a large crowd but there was no trouble. I do remember that, as her coffin was lowered into the ground, her sister Elizabeth became almost hysterical and she had to be led away.'

'Thank-you, Deputy Chief Constable, for your assistance. It is a most tragic tale.'

'Before you leave, Mr Hanozet, there is something more I should tell you in confidence about this case. I assume I can trust you?'

'Of course, Deputy Chief Constable. I assume that I cannot use this additional information until I have your agreement?'

'Precisely so. It is extremely sensitive at present and may well surprise you.'

'Please continue, sir. I do like a surprise.'

'Very well. A few months ago, a young lady from Farncombe, Eliza Hampton, went missing from her home. After an intense search, we found her body. It was buried in a shallow grave close to the very studio where Emily's body was found. Yes, it was in Mr Henderson's back garden. We carried out a thorough search of the area and found two other graves. Two more bodies. Yes, both were young ladies. One from Milford and one from Haslemere.'

'What was the reason for the search?'

'We had received information from a neighbour concerning Mr Henderson's, er, proclivities. He was arrested and duly confessed to a series of murders. One of those was of Emily Joy!'

'He admitted to killing Emily Joy? Even though Ebeneezer Jenkins had confessed?'

'Indeed. Mr Henderson said that he had been gardening on the evening of her death and heard shouting coming from the studio. He saw Mr Jenkins leaving and locking the door. He had a spare key so, once he was satisfied that he had gone, he opened the studio and found Emily Joy lying on the floor. He checked her pulse and found she was still alive. What he did next shocked even me – and I have 30 years' experience in the force. When Henderson had had his way with her, he smothered her. He said he assumed Mr Jenkins would return and conclude that he had,

250

indeed, killed her. But the next visitor wasn't him but the police. When Jenkins confessed to the murder, he assumed that he, Henderson, was now safe. Then, of course, his neighbour reported him and the other bodies were discovered. He decided he might as well admit to this additional murder as he was clearly going to hang. Best to clear his conscience, he said.'

'So Ebeneezer Jenkins was innocent after all?'

'Indeed he was. As you'll recall, he claimed insanity at his trial but that was rejected. Well, we've since spoken to his mother and a doctor who treated him. We have now concluded that he very likely was insane. He may well have hit Emily and, perhaps, knocked her out. But we are now satisfied that it was Henderson who killed her.'

'So it may be some time before this case goes to Court?'

'Very much so, Mr Hanozet. It promises to be an extremely complex matter. There may be many other victims.'

'So, to summarise, sir, it would be best to delay telling this story at present but, when all the facts are known…?'

'It might well be the subject of a book rather than a short story!'

Godalming Events

Victorian 1870 – 1901
1898 – Farncombe Station opened.
1897 – Borough Road Pumping Station built.
1894 – New drainage system established.
1892 – The Meath Home of Comfort for Epileptics (now called The Meath) opened.

PARKING PROBLEMS
by Paul Rennie

She pulled aside the lace curtains of her front room, peered suspiciously out over the low privet hedge to the road, and tutted through thin lips to herself. Yes, as she thought, there was another one. A red Ford Focus was reversing slowly into the parking space directly outside her house. Hilda Dibden had lived alone in the red brick semi-detached house in Town End Street, Godalming, for 53 years. It was once a small quiet street within walking distance to the shops and bright lights of the town, but with the advent of new housing development, multiple car ownership, double yellow lines, and the threat of traffic wardens and wheel clampers in other parts of the town, it had become congested with cars and a favourite free parking spot for people going shopping, or commuters heading to the station. The problem was that the Edwardian houses in Town End Street were built in days when there was no need for garages or driveways to park cars, and consequently space was at a premium. Mrs Dibden had never owned a car, but she considered that the kerb outside her house belonged to her, and woe betide anyone who had the temerity to occupy it.

She tore off her apron, and rushed outside to remonstrate with the car owner, but he was too quick for her. By the time she got to the street, the smartly dressed man in his fifties, with grey hair, had walked briskly away towards Brighton Road, and was already turning the corner. She went back inside, and every so often twitched the curtains to see if he was coming back, getting herself into her usual state of indignant anger. How dare he steal what was hers. This happened many times a day, and she was doggedly territorial about the space. She would rant at those who parked there, explaining that she needed that parking space for her visitors, although truth be told, she never had any because the way she glared out of the window with such a sour demeanour encouraged people to give her a wide berth. She didn't have much chance of making new friends, because she never went out, in case someone should sneak into the parking space when she wasn't watching.

She told those motorists who were prepared to argue with her that she had high blood pressure and needed the space kept clear in case there was an emergency, although, ironically, it was her obsession with the parking space that contributed to her high blood pressure. But still people continued to park outside her house, and her days were spent peering out and checking for space invaders. She had called Waverley Council many times to complain, but the Officer had patiently told her that nothing could be done. It was a public road and people had a right to park there, and the other residents needed somewhere to park their cars. She wasn't even allowed to put up a no parking sign. A couple of times she had put plastic garden chairs in the space, to deter parkers, but they were always moved, or once, disappeared completely.

She looked out of the curtains again. It was still there, the red car that seemed to be mocking her, saying, 'look at me I'm in your space'. A vein throbbed behind her eye. This was too much, the car had been there for at least an hour and a half. Perhaps the man had left it there while he went up to London. Maybe he had gone on holiday and the car could be there for weeks. She worked herself up into a frenzy. This was the last straw. If he wasn't coming back, she would have to take action. She would teach the driver not to park in her spot. She went to the sideboard and took out her sewing basket. In it was the bradawl she used for making holes in leather. She put it in her apron pocket and marched out of the front door, closing it behind her, and stood beside the offending car. She looked both ways along the street. As usual it was empty, apart from the line of cars. She took out the bradawl, pulled off the cork that protected its point, and bent down and stabbed the needle into the front tyre. There was a satisfying hiss as the tyre started to deflate. She could feel her heart pounding and the vein throbbing, but this was therapeutic. She moved to the rear and pushed the needle into the wall of the other tyre. Again there was a hiss, and the car did a little lurch as it leaned over onto its wheel rims.

As Hilda straightened up, she felt a slight pop somewhere inside her head, her vision went dark, her legs gave way and she fell to the ground. There she lay in a sprawled heap on the damp pavement. A few minutes later, the red car owner with the grey hair came back from his dental appointment. He saw the elderly lady lying beside his car and rushed over to help her. He knew enough first aid to realize immediately from the dilated pupil of her left eye and the way that side of her face drooped that she had had a stroke. He also knew that time was critical in getting a stroke patient treated to have the best chances of making a full recovery and avoiding permanent disablement or worse. He reached into his pocket for his mobile to call an ambulance, but then realized he had left it at home on the kitchen table, in case it fell out of his pocket while in the Dentist's chair. He looked around to see if there was anyone else around who might have a phone, but the street was deserted. Ah, perhaps he could ask the person in the nearest house to use their phone. He went to the door and rang the bell, but there was no reply, not surprising really, because Mrs Dibden was on the same side of the front door as he was. He tried another few houses along the street, but no-one seemed to be in.

There was nothing for it. Time was of the essence. He would have to drive her to Casualty himself. He opened the passenger door and tried as gently as possible to lift Mrs Dibden into the seat. She was quite a large lady, and it took a lot of time and effort to pull her up off the ground in her unconscious state and bundle her into the seat, and even longer to reach over her and connect the seat belt. He jumped into the driver's seat, turned on the engine and started to drive off. The steering felt oddly heavy and there was a flapping grinding noise from the passenger side. He jumped out again and went to look, and for the first time saw that both tyres were completely flat. The car wasn't going anywhere. In desperation he looked up and down the road again. Surely someone must come by, it was so close to a busy town.

Round the corner came a man on a bicycle, wearing a yellow jacket and black helmet. He waved frantically to the man to attract his attention. The cyclist cheerfully waved back, then turned up Carlos Street, never to be seen again. The road was deserted again. A few minutes went by and he checked on his passenger. She was still breathing, so no CPR was needed, but she was making slurred sounds. She needed treatment immediately. A young schoolgirl suddenly appeared near the car, peering alternately at her mobile phone and at the lady in the front seat. 'What's the matter wiv 'er, 'ad a few drinks?' she asked unsympathetically. 'No, I think she's had stroke, we need an ambulance,' said the driver. 'Can I use your mobile to call 999?' 'No battery,' said the girl, in a surly manner, and walked away.

The driver was getting increasingly worried. Another figure turned the corner and was coming towards him. It was a frail elderly lady in a long black coat, blue hat and surgical stockings, using a shopping trolley as a walking frame. He waited for her to reach the car, but she didn't seem to be getting any closer. She moved the trolley forward a couple of feet and after a long pause, moved her legs to catch up, then, after another pause, repeated the process.

257

She was going to take an eternity to reach him. He raced towards her to ask if she lived nearby. After all, she couldn't have travelled far from home. It turned out that she lived two doors down from the first house he had knocked on. He explained that there was a lady that had had a stroke and could he use her house phone to call for an ambulance. She agreed and they continued to edge slowly towards her house. 'I think we need to go quicker', said the man. 'Could you give me the keys, so that I can dash in?' 'I need to see your photo ID card,' said the elderly lady, 'You hear about those villains who trick their way into people's houses and steal their savings.' He didn't have anything on him that she would accept, so they continued their snail-like progress along the pavement. After about 5 minutes they reached the car, with Hilda still in the passenger seat. 'That's Hilda Dibden,' said the elderly lady. 'She and I fell out twenty years ago over parking in the street, when I used to own a car. Never speak to each other now.' After a few more minutes they eventually reached the house and the elderly lady, after fumbling for ages for her keys, went inside and passed the phone out to him on its cord. He was finally able to call 999, and to give them their due, the ambulance service arrived just inside its target time. Mrs Dibden was given an injection of clot buster drug by the paramedics, placed on a stretcher, and once loaded with its patient, the ambulance sped off to the Royal Surrey.

Six weeks later, Hilda was back at her home. The kindly carer brought over a cup with a fixed straw, and held it up to Mrs Dibden's lips. 'Here you are, Hilda, a nice cup of tea. It must be hard being stuck indoors all of the time, with no change of scenery. I'll move your wheelchair over to the front window so that you can watch the comings and goings outside. I'm sure you'll enjoy that. I'll open the curtains.' The patient made a gargling sound that the carer mistakenly took to be approval. Hilda stared out of the window through the one eye that she could focus.

A silver Audi was manoeuvring slowly into the parking space outside.

Godalming Events

Plantagenet 1154 – 1485
1440 – Robert Glover fined for exercising his craft whitening leather outside the Market Town.
1294 – Grant of Free Warren in the Manor of Godalming to Nicholas Longespee, Bishop of Salisbury.

THE CAT THAT GOT THE SAUCE

by Alan Barker

Microwave meal or Chinese takeaway? That was the burning question.

She stared at her empty coffee mug, struggling to reach a decision.

If she put a microwave meal in the oven now, she could start eating in five minutes. Whereas, a stroll to Farncombe village and back would take her half an hour.

Dr Wilkinson's words resonated through her mind: You're very healthy for your age, Virginia, but you must go for a brisk walk each day, preferably for at least 30 minutes. Above all, you need to get out and about, and it would also help if you found something positive to focus on.

She hadn't been out today due to the rain, but it had stopped now. And Thursday was always a good day to buy a Chinese takeaway as they offered a 20% cost reduction for old-age pensioners.

All right, she thought, so a plate of Chow Mein probably wasn't what Dr Wilkinson would have recommended. But at least she'd be undertaking a 30-minute walk, as her Fitbit would no doubt record.

At last, she made up her mind. It was a decision that would change the rest of her life.

'Number 46, please.'

'46!' the giant of a man behind the counter shouted to someone Virginia couldn't see.

Looking at the size of his paunch, she wondered whether he polished off all the leftovers.

Having paid for her meal, Virginia scooped up the carrier bag provided - really, she thought, I have no idea why they provide such a large bag for my tiny portion - and left the shop.

Outside she bumped into Fred, an acquaintance through their shared passion for Chinese food.

Having bemoaned the current state of the weather and his 'gammy' leg, Fred said, 'Can you check I've got the right money, love? The meal I ordered should come to £7.20 what with the 20% off, but my eyesight isn't so good these days.'

Virginia put down her carrier bag and checked the coins in the old man's hand before confirming he did indeed have the right amount. After a further exchange of pleasantries, she said that her food would be getting cold and she 'must dash.'

Back in her flat, she took a pre-heated plate from the oven and set it on the table. When she opened the carrier bag she found inside a tiny black kitten, curled up beside the Chow Mein, and fast asleep.

Virginia clapped a hand over her mouth and stared. She could only assume the kitten had jumped in the bag while she'd been chatting with Fred.

Carefully she reached into the bag, but as soon as she started lifting the meal the kitten awoke with a start and looked up at her, ears twitching.

'Where on earth did you spring from, poor little thing? Come on, let's get you out of there, shall we?'

Virginia opened a small tin of tuna and put the contents on a plate on the kitchen floor. The kitten tucked in greedily, and Virginia wondered when it had last eaten.

She had barely started on her own meal when the kitten jumped on the table, sniffing the food from several feet away. Gaining confidence, it inched closer and closer.

'This wasn't meant for you, little gannet. All right, we can share, if you like.'

Virginia put a spoonful of noodles between them. She watched as the kitten licked off the sauce, then sat up and looked at her as if to say: *Can I have some more?*

*****

The following morning Virginia typed a note to the effect that if anyone was missing a black kitten to contact her and she would be pleased to return it. She then distributed flyers around Farncombe and returned home to await results.

A week later no one had telephoned, and the kitten was treating the flat as its home.

'You can't stay here, I'm afraid,' Virginia said, tickling it under its chin. 'They don't like little pussy cats living in top floor flats. We'll just have to find you another home.'

*****

The next day Virginia made up a box and took the kitten to the nearest animal rescue centre.

Whilst waiting to be seen, it became apparent that a teenage boy further along the queue had a problem with his Dalmatian which was getting skittish and upset.

Leaving the kitten safely out of the way, Virginia asked the boy if she could help. Receiving his approval, she approached the Dalmatian very slowly, holding out her hand, fingers closed, palm down. The dog eyed her suspiciously, but after a while it stepped forward and sniffed her hand. A further short delay followed before the dog lowered its head and allowed her to stroke him.

'Hopefully he should be all right now,' she said to the boy.

A little later, the lady behind the counter said, 'You dealt with that Dalmatian extremely well.'

'I used to work as an assistant at the vet's in Godalming,' Virginia explained. 'I loved working with animals.'

The lady smiled. 'So, what have we got here then?' she asked, turning her attention to the kitten.

Virginia told her about the kitten worming its way into her flat, and that she hadn't received any response to her flyer.

'I don't suppose you know its name?'

'No, but I've started calling her Noodles. Please don't ask why,' Virginia said with a grin.

As she was leaving the centre with a heavy heart, having said 'goodbye' to Noodles, the lady she had been dealing with caught up with her and said: -

'I don't know if you would be interested but we are looking for volunteers to help out at the centre. No need to make a decision now, but here are our details in case you'd like to contact us.'

'Thank you,' Virginia said, her spirits rising. 'This is just what the doctor ordered!'

*****

A few weeks later, having submitted an application and attended a training session, Virginia was delighted to start work at the centre as a volunteer.

Noodles took a long look at her before mewing at the top of her little voice and running up to greet her.

Noodles was not impressed, however, when Virginia was asked to take Caesar, the Dalmatian, for his daily walk.

Arriving home later that afternoon, Virginia found a letter on her doormat. It was from the local authority and, on reading it, she clapped a hand to her chest in surprise.

In response to your recent application for a ground floor flat, we are pleased to inform you…

*****

Back at the rescue centre some weeks later, Virginia collared Noodles - who had been playing hard to get - and guided her into a cat box.

'I hope you're going to be on your best behaviour in your new home,' she said, tickling Noodles on the nose.

Once they arrived at the flat in Charterhouse Road - a ground floor property not far from Virginia's previous home, and with a view of the communal garden - Noodles set about exploring all the nooks and crannies, and then plopped herself on the sofa, purring loudly.

'Made yourself at home, have you? Then what shall we have for dinner - Chow Mein with lashings of noodle sauce, perhaps?'

CHRISTMAS GIFTS
by Christine Butler

On the eighth day of Christmas…

'Godalming 417123. Hello, is that Jack? I can't hear you very well, it's a bad line. What? Yes, that's better.

'Yes, thanks, I had a lovely Christmas though I missed you. Thank you for your unusual present. The label on the pot says it's a pear tree – is that right? It will look great on the patio.

'What? The bird in it? Well, it was dead so we roasted it for Boxing Day lunch. It was very tasty. No, I don't know why it was dead. Was it still alive when you handed the crate to the delivery people? Oh, poor thing, they should have fed it.

'Oh, the two doves fared better and were cooing in the garden for ages. We gave them some bird seed but it must have been the wrong sort because they flew away yesterday morning and haven't been back since.

'Yes, the hens are fine. We've penned them and have been feeding them with kitchen scraps. I'll buy some corn tomorrow. What? A fox? Ooh, I hadn't thought of that. Yes, yes, I'll get a proper coop for them, don't worry.

'The four calling birds were sweet. They didn't like the old canary cage we put them in, though, and

266

flapped about so much it upset our cat. She only caught one when she knocked the cage off the shelf. What's that? Yes, she ate it. At least the other three escaped. I heard them later in next door's garden.

'Thank you for the rings. Five, all different. They're lovely. And they fit, too.

'The geese? Oh, we penned them in with the chickens. Dad wanted to kill one to eat on New Year's Day but Mum and I wouldn't let him. By the way, how do you cook a goose egg? They're so big. Oh, Spanish omelette? I hadn't thought of that'

'The seven swans were a problem. As you know, our pond is only tiny. Didn't you think of that? I'm afraid Dad got cross with them, waddling all over the garden, and 'phoned Hydestile Wildlife Hospital for help. They're coming to get them shortly and will release them on Broadwater Lake.

'Yes, there'll be someone here for the rest of the day, to hand the swans over. Food for a party? I'll have to pop out to Sainsbury's. It will be lovely to see you but how many are you bringing with you and do I know them? Say that again? Eight milk maids, lords and ladies and a pipe and drum band? You're joking, of course?!'

MEET THE AUTHORS

Ian Honeysett

Aftcr reading Modern History at Corpus Christi College, Oxford and varied careers in Teaching (history & politics), Careers, Training & Human Resources, Ian decided to retire. Married to Jan, they have 3 children who live as far away as New Zealand, Witley & Farncombe. For 16 years he was a School Governor but has now retired from that too.

He currently devotes himself to writing (having co-written crime novels set in the French Revolution: http://goo.gl/Jecc7D), painting, editing (CLAN, a magazine for laryngectomees), military history, quizzes (he runs a U3A Quiz group with Jan), St Edmund's Parish work & playing the ukulele. Sometimes he even goes to the gym. No, really, he does. So, he's still fairly busy. He also quite likes to travel & has visited China, Japan, Australia, New Zealand, Canada, Alaska and Alderney in recent years. He has an interesting collection of waistcoats.

Martyn MacDonald-Adams

Martyn lives and works in Godalming. He is a lightly bearded, 1950s vintage, software development manager at a local financial services company. Apart from writing his other main hobby is composing songs and playing them in a local duo (called Nightingale Road), often for charity, to select groups polite enough to listen.

He sometimes dresses up in a Steampunk outfit because, he says, for the short time they're here, people take life far too seriously.

When he gets philosophical, he likes to muse on the fact that we *all* live together on the crust of a single, smallish, ball of molten rock - while it whizzes round and round a deadly nuclear fireball. Perhaps like the dinosaurs in the past, some of us look up into the sky, marvel at all the bright dots and hope that there's nothing substantial out there speeding toward us. Meanwhile, here we all are, poisoning our little home and squabbling amongst ourselves for reasons that he completely fails to understand.

Elif Tyson

Elif lived in the Godalming area for two short intervals during 2005 and 2006. Third time lucky she returned for good, and has lived here since late 2010. Elif is an Economist, and has many interests including a love of travelling and photography. She took up writing as a task to complete an unfinished project close to her heart, and in 2015 joined the GWG. That project is her late husband's novel and remains unfinished, but against all the odds, Elif tries and experiments, never giving up. Elif works full time, supports a charitable organisation and enjoys walks by the riverside with her dog, Sandy.

Louise Honeysett

Louise grew up in Farncombe, attending local schools and Godalming College before studying Maths at Durham University. She qualified as a chartered accountant before moving into the charity sector, working for UNICEF UK and then living in Cambodia for a year, working for a performing arts NGO. She is currently Director of Finance and Resources at the Cystic Fibrosis Trust. In her spare time Louise has been scout leader for 1st Coulsdon Scouts and also a member of the all-female barbershop chorus Surrey Harmony. When she's not doing any of those things, she generally has her nose stuck in a book.

Christine Butler

Christine Butler moved to Witley, just south of Godalming, in September 1980. At that time she and her husband Len had an old four-berth fibreglass Callumcraft cruiser moored on the River Wey at Farncombe Boathouse. She worked in Farnham, as a Personal Taxation Assistant in a bank, for many years. When she was made redundant in 2001, she joined a firm of accountants in Godalming, thus finishing her working life in the same town as it started in 1962. She didn't enjoy her first job at British Drug Houses' laboratories in Godalming and left after a few months.

Her main hobbies are family history and writing. When she retired in 2005, she took the opportunity to join an Adult Education Creative Writing course to learn about writing fiction rather than just articles for canal society and family history journals. Only once has she been paid for an article, so far. That was a piece for Evergreen Magazine about children's author Monica Edwards who lived in Thursley.

Pauline North

Pauline North grew up in the quiet countryside of West Sussex and was educated at Midhurst Grammar School and Guildford School of Art.

After her marriage to Brian, they lived briefly in Guildford before moving to the house in Binscombe where they still live.

Having worked in a wide variety of jobs, she answered an advertisement for 'An artistic person' and became a display artist. For eighteen years, Pauline worked as half of a two- woman team, creating and installing window displays across the south of England.

When, all those years later, it was time for a change, she opened a jewellery shop: *Sans Frontieres,* in Crown Court, Godalming. She recently closed the shop and now indulges in her passion for writing and has, so far, self-published two books:

Consequences (https://amzn.to/3cNFbBd)

…and Dusty Windows

Both are part of a series of romantic thrillers.

Pauline also enjoys painting, drawing, dressmaking and various other crafts.

Paul Rennie

Paul Rennie is a retired Health Care product development manager with time on his hands. In the 1980s, he gained a PhD in microbial biochemistry at Leeds University, and at the time was a world expert on armpits and body odour, an ideal qualification for running a launderette or for a ticket inspector on public transport. Things have moved on and he now spends his time playing golf, tennis, the guitar and ukulele, and sailing, all badly. Paul, his long-suffering wife Lesley and family, have lived on Frith Hill in Godalming for 24 years, and have a keen interest in local history.

Since retirement, he has taken up long distance walking with local friends, and has completed all 630 miles of the South West coastal path plus the South coast round to Margate, the Thames path and various canal routes. He has also bagged a few Munros and climbed Mounts Kilimanjaro, Kinabulu and

Toubkai, helped by a training regime involving the walk up Frith Hill from the Cricketers. Recently he was lucky enough to be on an expedition ship to Antarctica which set a record for reaching the furthest South of any previous passenger ship.

Many of Paul's stories are modern day cautionary tales, heavily influenced by Hilaire Belloc and Aesop's fables. Paul also specializes in writing letters of complaint. As a result, he is probably on a black list shared between the customer services departments of South-Western Trains, BT Broadband and most major consumer goods manufacturers.

He has all of his own teeth and hair.

David Lowther

David Lowther was born in Kingston but grew up in South Wales. He trained as a teacher at St John's College, York and worked in schools in the North and Midlands before retiring in 2008. Since then he has spent his time writing and watching films. Three of his novels: The Blue Pencil, Two Families at War and The Summer of '39, have been published by Sacristy Press of Durham as well as a non-fiction title, Liberating Belsen; Remembering the soldiers of the Durham Light Infantry.

David moved to Godalming with his wife Anne to be closer to their son's family at Kew Bridge in March 2017. He is a member of the British Film Institute, the Godalming Film Society and, of course, the Godalming Writers' Group.

Alan Barker

Alan is a retired tax accountant having spent most of his working life in Guildford and Godalming. Along with his wife Judy he now lives in Epsom within a horse's gallop of the racecourse, but retains strong links to Godalming and its surrounding area.

Following his retirement in 2018 Alan attended a creative writing course in order to pursue a lifelong ambition to write stories. He became a published author on 1 January 2019 and has since had various short stories and flash fiction stories published through competitions and magazines as well as Christopher Fielden's 'Writing Challenges'.

Alan's other pastimes include playing badminton and watching his beloved Woking FC.

Julie Buckingham

Julie is a child of the sixties. She grew up in Guildford, Surrey and was educated at George Abbot Girl's school. Married in the late 70's and with her family now grown-up, Julie has turned her hands to writing novels, painting animals and other interesting pictures, and practicing Reiki, achieving a moderate success in the healing art. She is also a fan of Yoga and Pilates. She has written Native American Indian history for the British School of Yoga, and has an adventurous fiction novel out now entitled They Walked Into Darkness - about the Cherokee Indians and the long march they were forcefully made to go on where many Indians died of cold and exposure to the elements.

Finally, if you have enjoyed reading Godalming Tales 3 (and we hope you have) then please leave a review on the Amazon & other book review sites.

Many thanks.

Printed in Poland
by Amazon Fulfillment
Poland Sp. z o.o., Wrocław